The Jerry McNeal Series

Always Faithful

(A Paranormal Snapshot)

By Sherry A. Burton

Dorry Press

The Jerry McNeal Series

Always Faithful
By Sherry A. Burton

The Jerry McNeal Series: Always Faithful
Copyright 2019
Originally published as: That Feeling: Always
Faithful Copyright 2016
by Sherry A. Burton
Published by Dorry Press
Photo by Hobbs Studio
Edited and Formatted by BZHercules.com
Cover by Laura J. Prevost
@laurajprevostphotography

ISBN: 978-1951386009

For more information on the author and her works, please see www.SherryABurton.com

A Special Thanks...

To my husband, Don, thanks for the fairytale. You truly are my Prince Charming.

To my daughter, Brandy, who calls me every day, just because.

To my editor and cover artist, you both are the best!

Many thanks to Tina, Becky, Tracie, Lisa, and Marie, for taking that one final look.

To my fans, thanks for the continued support!

Lastly, to my "voices," without whose help I would not be where I am. Thank you for giving me such amazing ideas.

In loving memory of my mother
Mary Juanita Lands, October 1942- May 2019,
who always loved "the story about the dog."

Prologue

September 8th, 1985

Jerry woke in the wee hours of the morning and rubbed a closed fist against his droopy eyes. It had been months since he'd awoken during the night, not since the time his gums were swollen and irritated, causing him to cry out in a desperate search of relief. He stuck his thumb in his mouth, chomped down, and felt nothing out of the norm. No pain that would have explained his being awake when all was quiet. His diaper was wet; maybe that was what had awoken him. He rolled onto his side, thinking to voice his concerns to his mother and stopped, once again jamming his thumb into his mouth. Something was wrong, but it had nothing to do with his diaper. He focused his attention on the lamp at the far side of the room. A small glow emitted from the lamp, which sat atop a tall brown chest of drawers. He'd seen that same lamp every time he woke, and while it looked the same, in the wee hours of this Sunday morning, a feeling told him there was something different about it. A feeling that the lamp needed watching. Eyes wide, he did just that. Watched. Lying perfectly still except for his mouth, which worked greedily at his right thumb. Jerry, a thumb sucker since birth, had rejected pacifiers for something more tangible. Of course, he didn't realize the particular advantages of thumb sucking at first, but they'd become clear after several of his playmates were made to give up their own, less permanent devices. Not Jerry. No siree. His was always there at the ready whenever he felt the need for comforting, like at present when something was most assuredly wrong. His mouth tugged at his thumb as he waited, slurping a silent vigil in the darkness for what was about to happen.

He didn't have to wait long.

Within minutes, the wall beside the dresser lit up in a flash of white. Jerry watched in absolute amazement as the bright light traveled from the wall to the lamp. It made a sound like when his mommy was in the kitchen fixing him something to eat. He'd never seen anything so bright. He could feel the warmth coming from the cord. Cords were not supposed to be hot. If they were, his mother would not have let him anywhere near the lamp. He smelled something. It didn't smell like anything his mom had cooked. He wasn't sure what it was, but he didn't like it. He pulled his blanket over his head with his free hand, trying to make the bad smell go away. He wanted his mommy and daddy, but he couldn't see them. The bright light was traveling up the curtains. It was pretty and made the room bright enough to see. The room was empty. It was also very hot. As the heat intensified, he grew more and more afraid. He wasn't sure what that bright light was, but he didn't like it.

Jerry woke from the dream with a strangled cry. He looked out through the bars of his crib, peering out into the darkness. His trusty thumb was stuck securely between his lips, and from the wrinkled texture had been in place for most – if not all – of the night. The lamp that had been drenched in flames only moments before was soft and illuminating. Everything seemed to be as it should be, but he had a feeling it would not be that way for long. It was the first of a long history of what he would come to know as *that feeling*. A knowing that he would embrace, and something that would shape the core of the man he would someday become. For the moment, at eleven days past his second birthday, Jerry was utterly and desperately afraid of that which he could not control.

Where are Mommy and Daddy? I need them.

Chapter One

Holly squinted through the lens, waited for precisely the right second when the bride was between breaths, then, *snap*, captured the photo. She turned the screen to admire her handiwork and sighed, knowing this photo would soon replace the one that was currently showcasing the main page on her website. It was a perfect photo, with the quintessential perfect fairytale couple. The bride's long dark hair was upswept, held in place with a delicate halo of baby's breath flowers and one single red rose. Thin dark wisps of hair hung in tiny ringlets along the sides of her temples, her natural beauty made even more striking by the daring use of bold makeup around her equally dark eyes. The bride's lips had been shaded to match the color of her rose, lending a storybook feel to the photograph, both standing out boldly against the paleness of her skin. Bare milky white shoulders gave way to the intricate lace of her pearly white gown, which hugged her body like a second skin. If the bride had intended to channel Snow White, she had most assuredly obtained her goal. The groom, equally handsome, stood out in an ink-black tuxedo, with waves of dark flowing hair and mischievous brown eyes, which seemed to say *I've found my princess and I cannot wait to have my way with her*. Holly had the couple turn and positioned the groom's hands so they splayed across the small of his new wife's back, fingers placed just so, forming a perfect heart. Several members of the bridal party made comments of approval as they moved to see Holly's placement of the newlyweds. She took a photo, then snapped several more just to be certain, before checking the camera and nodding her satisfaction. People hired her to capture memories; what she gave them was perfection. Images to last a lifetime, or at least until they burned said pictures during a nasty divorce. *Not this couple; this couple will beat the odds.* At least that was what Holly told herself. Of course, she said the same thing about every wedding she photographed. It was her motto at her photography studio, giving every couple enchanting photos that would follow them into their happily ever after.

Barf!

She bit her lower lip to keep from gagging and moved to her left to get a better angle, all the while chastising herself for being so cynical. She pressed the button with her index finger, silently wishing the couple many years of happiness. Something she found difficult to do, since she herself stopped believing in happy endings at the tender age of twelve. The age she'd been when her parents had divorced. Up until that point, she'd thought life perfect, her family perfect. *Nothing's perfect.*

She bent sideways, *except this photo*, she thought

and pressed the button to capture the picture. She marveled at how beautiful Morgan, the bride, looked. *I wonder if I would look as beautiful.* Not likely, given the fact she was more comfortable in little to no makeup, jeans, and t-shirts, most likely imprinted with the logo from her website. Hollywood Films, a genius play on her first and last name, Holly Wood. Hey, what could she say, wherever she went, she was assured free advertising. Well, after the cost of the initial printing. Not today, though. Today, she was impeccably dressed to blend in. That was why she'd spent nearly an hour straightening her mane of thick brown hair, only to ruin the whole process by twining the entire mass of hair into a long braid, which rounded her head and draped across her right shoulder. *Maybe I should have added some baby's breath to the braid.* A sudden image of Rapunzel standing next to Snow White floated through her mind. She almost laughed and caught herself. *Get a grip, Holly. It's a long way till midnight, and you still have to film the ball.* This time, she did snicker.

Morgan turned to her, the full-length gown following after her in a trail of shimmering elegance. "Is something wrong?"

Just tell the truth. "No, I just found myself wondering if I'd make as beautiful of a bride as you and, well…" She lifted the braid, then spread her fingers and watched as it fell limp against her shoulder.

"Of course you would, wouldn't she, Grant?"

Morgan said, smiling over her shoulder at her new husband.

Grant, who'd obviously been listening, leaned in and spoke in hushed tones, "You are a very lovely lady and, to prove it, I'll have you know my best man has already been making inquiries as to how well I know you." He wiggled his eyebrows at her before nodding towards the opposite side of the room.

Holly casually turned in the direction of where the rest of the wedding party was standing, patiently waiting for her to call them when needed. In the center of the throng was the best man, a tall, lean, and incredibly handsome twenty-something man currently doing handstands while the others cheered him on.

"He's got stamina," Grant said, and the three of them laughed.

"Good to know," Holly said and wondered what else he was good at. Feeling a blush spreading over her, she shook off her curiosity and motioned the duo into another pose.

Just what I need, another child.

Morgan was now holding her bouquet of blood-red roses that matched both her lips' color and the single red rose that Grant wore in his lapel. She was leaning into her new husband in a stance that looked as if they were already comfortable with one another. Like a pair that truly fit together and, now that they were joined, only good things would come their way. As she peered through the camera lens, the newly married Mr. and Mrs. Bilkner looked just like one of those fairytales that she touted on her website, yet she no longer believed in. Holly took the photo and heaved a sigh.

Oh well, let them have their moment and the pictures to prove they were once happy. Lowering the camera, she plastered a smile onto her face. "Okay, let's get the rest of the wedding party over here so we can create some memories."

She snapped a few candid photos as the bridal party took up positions around the happy couple. She liked to sneak these unplanned snapshots to the photograph package at no extra charge. It was what made her sessions special, what got people talking, and what led her to be highly sought after when it came to location shoots. Her reputation was as one of the best, not only in Chambersburg, the Pennsylvania town in which she lived, but the surrounding towns as well. It was what had brought her to Gettysburg today, during one of the worst snowstorms of the season. *Blizzard,* she reminded herself. She took a deep breath, letting it out slowly as she changed the camera lens. The evening had only just begun, and the snow, which had been falling all day, was not projected to stop until well after her current gig was over. It wouldn't be the first time she'd driven in heavy snow. Still, she'd taken precautions, borrowing her father's Jeep – it was older, but had 4-wheel-drive and was much more dependable than her Mustang. *No use worrying about things you can't change*, she thought, raising the camera. She focused on the bride and groom, who seemed to radiate happiness.

Maybe this couple will actually beat the odds.

"Hold still, everyone," Holly called, then pressed the button to freeze the moment forever. The best man, a handsome fellow with pearly white teeth and a devilish smile, closed his eyes just as she'd snapped the photo. He must have realized this, as he made eye contact with her and shrugged an apology.

Flirt! You're too young, and I'm too not interested. At thirty, the last thing she was looking for was a guy whose idea of fun was doing handstands with a rose clenched between his teeth. While the guy might have stamina, he didn't exude much in the maturity department. And that carried a lot of weight. Especially since she had her daughter, Gracie, to consider.

"Do over. Let's all try to keep our eyes open this time," she teased and waited for everyone to return to their previous positions. She continued to pose people and take photos for another twenty minutes before finally releasing the group, most of which whooped with delight as they gathered their belongings and began making their way downstairs to the reception area. Thankfully, the reception was being held in the basement of the church. A lucky break, given the weather conditions – at least she wouldn't have to venture outside until it was time to leave. Holly disconnected the wide-angle lens, then stuffed it into her bag. She'd just turned to follow the group when Morgan came up beside her, her face flushed against her milk-white skin. She seemed hesitant.

"Is something wrong?"

Morgan's blush deepened. "No, I…well… I was just hoping… I know it is probably impractical, but I saw this photo on Pinterest and, well, I was hoping to recreate it."

Pinterest had taken scrapbooking to a whole new level. A person could find virtually anything on there from recipes to hairstyles, to gardening tips and more. The possibilities were endless. Once found, you "pinned" the photo to your board and could come back to it anytime you were ready. No tape, no glue, no mess; all you needed was internet access and a surfing device, such as a cell phone or computer.

"Got to love Pinterest," Holly agreed.

"Totally," Morgan said brightly. "It's where I got most of my ideas for the wedding. Some people are so creative."

"I'm not sure how any of us survived without it," Holly replied. "I use it all the time myself."

"I know! That's where I got the idea from, one of your boards."

"Really?" Holly asked, wondering what photo she'd picked and just how risqué as to make for the proverbial blushing bride. "Does it include nudity?"

"I hope so," Grant said, stepping up behind Morgan and placing his hands on her bare shoulders.

She laughed and leaned into him. "Not even so much as cleavage."

He started to plant a kiss on top of her head before settling on the nape of her neck instead, careful to avoid the clips that held her hair in place. "Ah well, there's plenty of time for that later."

Morgan's blush deepened. Any redder and Holly would have to do some serious airbrushing to remove the color. "So tell me which picture you're referring to."

"I know it sounds crazy, but I'd like to take a picture in the snow. You know, the one where the bride looks like she's standing in a snow globe?"

So much for not going outside.

Holly knew exactly which photo Morgan was envisioning, and how unattainable it would be in the current weather conditions, since she'd taken the photo herself. The bride, a young woman named Kathy, was standing in the middle of a beautiful snow-covered garden while soft flakes of white flowed around her. The difference was, she'd taken the photo in broad daylight, and the snow had only just started to fall. The sun had filtered perfectly through the snow, and nary even the slightest breeze had lifted the air. All the planets had aligned, giving Holly the perfect setting for the illusion. And it was an illusion, one that could not possibly be duplicated in blinding snow with driving winds. She had also seen the look of determination in Morgan's eyes; she'd be wasting her time trying to reason with the woman. No, some things are better shown. It wouldn't take much, a wintery blast up the delicate gown, or wind tugging at her perfectly fashioned hair. It was little things such as this that guaranteed her future referrals. Not snow, nor sleet, nor wind, nor hail. Holly herself had come from a long line of letter carriers who used to chant that very slogan, all the while wishing they were home with the rest of the world instead of tramping through the elements. Besides, she was reasonably sure this would be her fastest outdoor session ever.

"I'm willing to give it a try if you are," she said, tugging on her coat, motioning towards the door.

Chapter Two

Fingertips pressed together in prayer formation, Trooper Jerry McNeal stared idly at the blank wall of his cubicle. He'd been in the same position for nearly half an hour. It wouldn't be long now before he felt the need to explore. He stood and walked the short distance to the window, at first seeing nothing but the reflection of his shaved head. He leaned closer, peering into the night, watching as snow whirled past the streetlights like an angry swarm of hornets. His breath, warm against the window caused the glass to fog, yet he didn't seem to notice. He was no longer looking at what lay beyond the glass but listening to something no one else could hear. It was a night where he'd rather remain indoors, a night where he wished others would do the same. "If only," he said to the fogged glass. Turning from the window, he started towards his chair, moved to sit, thought better of it, and began pacing the confines of the room instead. He never knew when *the feeling* would show up, but it was here now, and he was listening.

Waiting.

For what, he was not sure. He normally never knew what *it* was until it happened. The feeling was a part of him. A part that told him he was not like everyone else. His grandmother – an Appalachian mountain woman – always told him it was a gift from the gods. His mother referred to it as his super-power. She'd said she first knew he was special when he'd woken in the night screaming the words "HOT! HOT!" A few moments later, his mother was standing beside his crib, still trying to comfort him when she'd smelled smoke and saw a white cloud drifting upwards into the room. A frayed cord on a lamp in Jerry's room had faltered, starting a fire on the upper level. The batteries in the family's smoke detectors were long dead, and no warning had come from the neglected device. All inside would have perished, starting with Jerry himself, if Jerry had not woken them with his cries. That was the first time he could remember having had *that feeling*. He had just turned two years old.

A snowy image flittered through his mind. He sighed. Of course, there would be snow; the whole state and most of the surrounding region was under a blizzard warning. The accumulation had been mounting all day. Roads were already impassable in many areas. Even the state police post was running on a skeleton crew, many of its officers not able to leave the confines of their driveways. He shook off his frustration and continued to pace the small office space. A blinding flash made him stop to gather this second piece of the puzzle. *A transformer, maybe?* He didn't think so. A transformer blowing would not be optimal during current weather conditions, but he didn't think such an event would warrant his increased restlessness. No, this was the type of feeling he normally got when human lives were at stake, the type of feeling that inspired him to become a Pennsylvania State Police Trooper when his enlistment ended with the Marines. He'd thought the Marines would be a good fit, and it was. At first. Then his second deployment changed all that. His feelings were on hyper-alert as every day something bad happened. While Iraq might be a good place for a Marine looking for a bit of excitement, it was not the place for a Marine with a special gift that would warn him when something bad was going to happen. It was Iraq, and there was a war going on. Something bad was always happening. The problem was that knowing something was going to happen and being powerless to stop it was enough to nearly drive him mad. While he'd managed to keep from going insane, the feeling had driven him away from the Marines. Thankfully, he had found a new home, which now allowed him to help when the feeling showed him the way. This evening, that feeling seemed to be on hyperdrive.

It's going to be bad, whatever it is.

Jerry moved down the hall and into the breakroom. Once there, he circled the room like an animal trapped in a cage, his anxiety piquing until he finally decided he had to leave the room or scream. He opted for leaving the room, knowing full well screams would lend way to panic and drawn weapons as his comrades raced to his aid. Instead, he tugged on his heavy black coat and rooted in his pockets for his gloves, pulling them on as well. With a heavy sigh, he headed for the outer office, smiling sheepishly at the bewildered stares of his fellow troopers.

Sergeant Seltzer leaned back in his chair, eyeing Jerry with a cross between wonder and awe. "Jesus, McNeal, you're not actually going out in this crap, are you? Tell me you're just going out for a smoke."

Jerry cast the older man a look he was sure mimicked the man's puzzled face. "We both know I don't smoke."

"I know, but I was hoping you had suddenly decided to start."

"Beats the alternative, doesn't it?"

"Might."

Jerry was fairly certain Seltzer had been a cop in his previous life, as well as the one before that. The man had a look about him. One that said, "I've seen it all." Suddenly, an image of an old-time sheriff came to mind: same white hair, only longer, smoothly pushed back under a Stetson hat, as well as a double-barrel shotgun lazily draped across his jean-clad lap, matching pearl-handled pistols freshly polished and ready for use. For an instant, Jerry expected the man to turn and spit the juice from what he was chewing into a waiting spittoon. The image cleared as the station commander blew a bubble; the tobacco replaced with chewing gum, jeans with a deep gray regulation uniform, pistol – singular – planted firmly in its holster. Jerry rolled his neck to release the tension. Obviously, fresh air would do him some good.

Sergeant Seltzer leaned forward, his white hair shining brightly in the overhead fluorescents. "I take it you've seen the weather reports. Franklin County just went under a state of emergency. No one on the roads unless it's essential."

Jerry removed his gloves and filled his travel mug with coffee, twisting the plastic lid tightly against the rim. "When did that ever stop people from their stupidity?"

"You know we don't have enough manpower to double up, much less send someone along on a joy ride."

Jerry gave an involuntary shudder. "Let's hope that's all this turns out to be."

Seltzer met his eyes. "Not likely, though, is it, son?"

"No."

"So you got a destination in mind or just going for a drive?" Sergeant Seltzer asked. He sighed and made to reach for his brimmed hat.

Jerry waved a hand in dismissal. "No use both of us freezing our asses off. The feeling's not urgent. Just enough to make me want to take a drive."

It was a lie, as the feeling had been blaring like a siren for hours, but something about this one felt different. More personal.

Seltzer looked relieved. "Well, all the same, take Manning's SUV. He's still on leave, and your cruiser's no match for this storm. Check in with dispatch as soon as you figure out what direction you're headed. I'd rather have a heads up if I have to send anyone out."

When, Jerry thought. *When you have to send others out. Soon, but not yet.*

Jerry nodded in agreement before plucking the keys from the board. He squeezed them gently, sending a silent condolence to Manning, who had been on leave since the loss of his partner seven days earlier. Bracing against the wind, Jerry opened the door stepping out into the swirling chill. He picked his way carefully across the parking lot towards the row of SUVs, using the key fob to find his way. He brushed the snow from the windshield with his gloved hand, thankful it was a dry snow. After buckling his seatbelt, he started the SUV to let the engine warm, closed his eyes, and listened. He likened it to a homing device; only the device was his body. The feeling would pull at him, much like a game of Hot or Cold. If he were moving in the right direction, it would just feel right. If not, the clutter inside his head would grow until he turned around and silenced it. Try explaining that to a medical doctor. "You have a gift," one MD had told him.

"No, I have a feeling," he'd replied.

"Yes, but that feeling is a gift."

"Call it what you want. Just give me something to make it go away."

The doctor had stared at him in disbelief. "Surely you jest."

"Yeah, Doc. I just came from a fatal accident.

One that I knew about before it happened, yet was powerless to do anything to stop. I always joke about shit like that." He hadn't meant to take out his frustrations on the poor guy, but it had been an extremely difficult day. A mother and her unborn child had died, and there was nothing Jerry could have done to prevent it. That was the same reason he'd walked away from the Marine Corps when he was nearly halfway through to retirement. People died, and there was nothing he could do about it. Knowing something was going to happen didn't usually stop it from happening. Sure, sometimes the gift would clue him in well in advance, and he could route his men in a different direction, but more often than not, he was kept in the dark until his services were needed. He got out because he was tired of being the freaking cleanup crew.

The doctor had moved to the sink to wash his hands. There was a calmness in the way the man stood there staring at the water coming from the faucet. Methodically, he ran his hands under the rushing water, then reached for the soap dispenser. As the soap bubbled within his palms, he turned his face to Jerry and spoke. "I have a gift."

The words had so shocked Jerry that he had jerked his head up in surprise.

"Oh, not the kind you have. But do you think mine is all that different?" The doctor turned off the faucet, pulled two paper towels from the holder, and began to dry his hands. "I went to medical school. With a simple exam, or not so simple medical test, I can make a diagnosis. The majority of the time, I'm correct and can, as you said, make it all go away. But for the others, I'm left feeling helpless, wondering why I bother. Would you have me give up helping those I can because of those I cannot?" The doctor tossed the towels into the trash and left the room before Jerry could reply.

Damn. The doctor was good.

That was six years ago. Jerry had just celebrated his first year on the job. A few days earlier was when he'd gotten a feeling, been led to the scene, only to find there was nothing he could do. He'd felt once again that he was simply part of the cleanup crew and was considering putting in his resignation yet again. Since that time, no matter the outcome, Jerry had never questioned his gift. He was currently serving his seventh year as a Pennsylvania State Trooper.

Jerry put the SUV into gear, crept to the edge of the parking lot, hesitated, and then took a left towards the interstate. Once at the main intersection, he moved to merge onto Interstate 81. At the last second, he whipped the wheel, nearly spinning in a complete circle and headed left towards US Route 30 instead. Apparently, he was now heading in the right direction, as his hands relaxed against the steering wheel. Sometimes, the feeling would begin before the trouble even existed. He was pretty certain this was one of those times.

Chapter Three

Dennis Young looked into the worried eyes of his wife of nine years. Lifting his hand, he smoothed the crease between her dark eyes. "Get rid of that," he said softly.

Selina managed a smile. "It's always hard to see you leave on nights like this."

"I know, but try to remember I'm driving the safest thing on the road," he said, speaking of the county snowplow truck he drove. He felt her sigh as he wrapped his arms around her, pulling her as tight as both their enormous stomachs would allow. They'd had this same conversation nearly every time he headed out to work. Dennis tried to soothe her the best he could, which was not easy. His Latino wife was extremely superstitious and exceedingly hormonal, both of which had him walking on eggshells of late. Not totally her fault, but not the best combination for the husband of a fiery woman in her last trimester of pregnancy.

"I know. I just have a bad feeling tonight," Selina said softly.

He laughed. "You always have a bad feeling, and yet I manage to come home every time."

She made a halfhearted attempt to pull away

from him. "Stop teasing me. I'm your wife. The mother of your children. Am I not allowed to worry? I'm your wife; it's my job."

"Yes, you are allowed." He kissed her on the temple. "And you're very good at it."

"I'm also very good at this," she said, placing her mouth on his.

Her lips were soft and warm. He'd love more than anything to be able to explore them in more detail, but he was already running late. Reluctantly he pulled away and placed a hand on her protruding belly. "I promise to stay safe, Mamacita."

"You'd better," she said, turning from him.

He followed her into the kitchen and watched as she pulled several bags from the fridge, placing each carefully inside his lunchbox. It was a child's lunchbox with a likeness of Superman on the outside, his Father's Day present from his boys, Cory and Cooper, twin seven-year-olds. They'd picked it out themselves, saying he was their hero. When he'd asked them why, they said *it was because he kept the roads safe for everyone to drive on.* He smiled as he did every time he remembered how excited they were at finding him the perfect gift. They had dashed into his room upon waking, smiling matching missing-tooth grins – they'd both lost the same front tooth only one week before – begging him to open the package. *Please, Papa, don't wait. You must open it now!* He was a lucky man to have such an amazing family. To them, he *was* their Superman. Who needed a cape when you had a sixty-thousand-pound truck at your disposal?

Selina closed the lunchbox and peered at him, her gaze serious. "You have a turkey sandwich with mustard and lettuce. Celery and carrots and hummus and just because I know you, there is a slice of angel food cake," she said, handing him the case.

"I bet Superman was never on a low-fat diet," Dennis said, frowning at the bag.

This brought a smile to her face.

"That's because Superman didn't have high cholesterol." She reached for his medication. Opening the container, she handed him a small pill.

"I bet Superman didn't get treated like a baby."

"Si, but Superman doesn't have a belly to match his pregnant wife's either. You do. Besides, Superman would likely remember to take his pills."

A low blow, followed by a direct hit. Both painful but also painfully true. Dennis was overweight to begin with, and his weight had steadily increased as Selina's pregnancy progressed. At first, Selina hadn't mentioned it, but then Dennis had developed heart palpitations. A trip to the doctor showed that Dennis was well on his way to a heart attack if he didn't make some serious changes. One of those changes meant lowering his cholesterol. This was to be accomplished by diet and medication. Medication that Dennis didn't remember to take, which was the precise reason why his wife had taken over dispensing the pills. He opened his mouth, waiting for Selina to place the pill on his tongue before washing it down with the remnants of his coffee. His wife blew out a sigh, then placed the pills back on top of the fridge.

"I'm pretty sure the bottle says to take with water," she said, turning to him.

"I took it with water. It just happened to be flavored with coffee grounds," he said gruffly.

Selina leveled a look at him. "Just make sure you eat the lunch I prepared. No stopping at the drive-thru."

"It's a blizzard out there. I doubt anything is open," he reminded her.

Her eyes narrowed in response.

"Yes, Mom," he said, and stuck out his tongue. At least in his head. He would not dare provoke the woman standing in front of him any more than necessary. Being treated like a child was bad enough, but his wife could punish him much more effectively than his mother ever could. Sleeping on the couch was just the beginning. Taking away other more intimate things was something he'd rather avoid. He pressed his lips together in remembrance of her recent kiss. "Turkey, rabbit food, and a slice of angel food cake given to me by my angel," he replied instead.

"No stopping at Rutter's either," she said, referring to one of the local gas stations along his route.

Before he could think of a witty reply, his radio crackled, then announced that the roads were worsening and reminded everyone that they were still under a state of emergency. Seeing the worry lines crease her face, he sat his lunch on the counter and folded his arms around her once more.

"See there; we are under a state of emergency. There won't be anyone on the roads but me." She chuckled in response. They both knew that not everyone heeded weather-related warnings. "That's better, Lina. You know I hate leaving you, but it's my job, and I happen to be pretty darn good at it."

He lifted her chin with a gentle hand and lowered his mouth to hers. What he thought would be a simple peck in farewell turned steamy and left him hungry for more. Mood swings were only a small portion of things that had increased during her pregnancy. Though Selina had always been eager, she had been rabid with a heightened sex drive since the beginning of her unplanned pregnancy, a tricky thing as both their stomachs expanded. He glanced at the kitchen clock. *Way too late to call in sick.* He wondered, momentarily, if it would help to just tell the truth. As far as he knew, no one on his crew had ever called in horny. It would probably earn him hero status with all the guys as well. Thinking better of it, he picked up his lunchbox and headed for the door.

***

The short drive to work proved Selina's fears to be valid. The snow was already well over a foot deep, and that was on top of several feet that were already on the ground. While the snow on the roads was not as deep as on the fields, it was plenty deep enough to wreak havoc on the roadways, and the white stuff was not showing any signs of letting up anytime soon. It would be all the plows could do just to keep up. He'd used the plow on his Jeep Wrangler to make his way the short distance from his house off Duffield Road to the county garage on Highway 997 to pick up his work truck, an impressive yellow beast he'd named Hercules. It was midnight when Dennis officially began his shift. Normally, he'd do eight hours and be done, but for a storm this size, the shifts had been expanded to twelve on twelve off, with trucks running around the clock. The trucks were well maintained and could handle the added demand. A plus to rotating the trucks, his truck was warm and ready when he arrived. As Hercules idled, he checked all the gauges. Next, he tilted the blade, checking the readings on his monitors for any issues. Finding everything in order, he said a short prayer and moved to the loading area to get his truck filled with a mixture of calcium chloride and salt. He watched in the large side mirror as Pete, the loader driver, maneuvered the Caterpillar into position, lowered the bucket into the pile, and moved forward. Once the bucket was full, he lifted the contents into the air, carefully positioning it over the edge of the dump bed before tilting the scoop. The truck jerked as the contents landed, then settled with a final shiver.

Pete's voice drifted through the radio, speaking over the rumble of the truck. "That will do it for now."

Dennis keyed the mike of his radio. "Thanks, man. I'm off to make the streets safe for all those who dare to venture out."

"Yeah, you and a dozen others. Stay safe out there. I'll catch you on your return."

Dennis pulled to the edge of the parking lot, lowered the blade, and took a left onto Highway 997. The truck burrowed a path along the winding road that led to US Route 30 – also known as Lincoln Highway. He caught a green light at Rutter's and made an easy right onto Lincoln Highway and began clearing his official route – US Route 30 from the borough's edge to the Franklin/Adams county line. He'd turn around just the other side of the county line in the Adams County lot, then make his way back to the edge of the borough before doing it all again, only deviating when time to reload the truck. Monotonous to some, but not to him; he knew this road like the back of his hand. Knew every curve, hill, and hidden driveway. Knew when he needed to slow down and exactly what speed to maintain to make the clearest path, providing people stayed out of his way. With a few exceptions, businesses were closed, even those that normally remained open throughout the night. He preferred it this way; it was much easier and safer than to slam on the brakes when a car pulled out in front of him. Obviously, most people did not realize what was involved in stopping a fully loaded salt truck. As if on cue, a Chevy Tahoe pulled out in front of him. Dennis managed to get the truck stopped just in time to avoid crashing into the rear of the SUV. He wondered at his wife's feeling. *Don't get jumpy, Dennis. She's just on edge right now. Worried about the baby is all.* They'd both been, as it seemed another child was not in the cards for them. They'd tried for years after the boys; two pregnancies followed, and neither made it to term. Then years went by with nothing happening. Dennis and Selina had resigned themselves to being a family of four. Each had gained weight and settled into a comfortable routine. For Dennis, that included work and joining the family at soccer practice when his schedule allowed. For Selina, it involved all the wifely and motherly duties and a newfound love of cooking and baking, which was what had led to some of the family's weight issues. Selina had not even known she was pregnant until the second trimester. By then, the doctors said she had a high chance of making it to full term. They both knew this baby would most likely be their last, so both were anxious for her to be born. Each had been thrilled to learn the child Selina was expecting was a girl. Dennis tried hard to picture a small replica of his wife, with rich brown skin and eyes the color of coffee. Or would she resemble the boys with their olive tones? Maybe she would surprise them all and come out looking like Dennis, pasty white with green eyes. *For her sake, I hope not.* He smiled. *All I know is, she's going to be beautiful.*

Hercules muscled its way east, throwing a

rooster tail of snow in its path. Dennis listened to the mindless chatter on his work radio and settled in for the long night ahead. He passed Rutter's with only a side glance. He had a turkey sandwich and willpower. Not really. He'd had a green light. That willpower could very well have been tested if the light had been red. He would pass this way many more times before his shift was through. Chances were pretty decent that said willpower would be tested numerous times over the course of the night.

Chapter Four

The lights of the reception room blinked: one, two, three times. The third wink kept the room dark for several seconds before illuminating the basement once more. Cheers erupted from the wedding guests, whoops and hoorays all joyfully echoing off the painted concrete walls of the church basement. While Holly was pleased the lights had withstood the latest wintery blast, she was pretty sure that would not remain the case much longer. She looked around to see if anyone shared her thoughts. She made eye contact with Sandy, the mother of the bride, and was relieved to see a look of resignation on the woman's face. Sandy shrugged and glanced at the lights as if asking for confirmation.

Holly nodded her agreement and felt guilty after having done so. While she was pretty sure the power would be out shortly, ending the event, she would prefer that end to come sooner than later and was more than ready to be home. She'd had an uneasy feeling ever since she'd followed Morgan and Grant outside a few hours earlier. While she'd known it had been snowing the entire time they'd been inside, she was surprised at just how much snow had fallen since she'd arrived. Driving home would be interesting, to say the least.

"Okay, people, I think that's our warning," Sandy shouted above the cheers. "Let's wrap this up before we lose power completely."

Thank God, Holly thought and then felt better at hearing the mumbles of agreement from others in the room. She took one final picture, then set to work breaking down her camera equipment, carefully removing the lenses and placing them between the dividers of her camera bag. One of the dividers had come loose. Instead of wasting time with it, she pulled her knit hat out of her coat pocket and placed the camera inside. *Just call me Miss MacGyver,* she thought and zipped the bag shut. *Not too bad with a camera either, Miss Mac*, she added, taking a mental inventory of some of the photos she'd taken. She'd been stalking the partygoers for hours, finding them unaware and capturing random photos that would fill albums and, God-willing, delight the bride and groom for years to come.

It was well past midnight; the bride and groom had already departed, slipping out unnoticed. Or so they thought. She had noticed and had the picture to prove it. She didn't always stay on the job this long, but the bride's parents had paid for the deluxe package. Normally, the late hour wouldn't be such a big deal, but they were under a blizzard warning, and she still had a twenty-three-mile drive home. Eighteen-plus inches was the expected total, at least the last time she'd had a chance to check the news. They were well on their way. At least ten inches of the white stuff had made it to the ground the last time she'd peeked outside. That was over two hours ago. She'd just finished packing her supplies when Sandy approached her.

"Are you sure you don't want to spend the night?" She was still wearing the taupe dress she'd worn to the wedding but had removed the heels and covered her stockings with thick wool socks that stretched the length of her slender calves. Her dark hair was still pulled up, but strands had fallen, and others strained against the pins that held them in place. She smelled of a mix of perfume and alcohol, and was well past tipsy, but Holly didn't think she would be considered drunk. Relaxed, yes – maybe for the first time in months – tired – most assuredly – but not drunk. Holly had heard the woman extend the same offer to others over the last few moments – some had taken her up on her hospitality, and others declined, saying they had made other arrangements. Sandy looked about ready to drop, not unusual for a haggard mother of the bride, but her smile was warm, the invite genuine. Holly thought about taking her up on her offer but just couldn't bring herself to say yes.

"Thank you for the offer, but I'm going to have to pass. I promised my daughter that I'd be there in the morning when she woke up."

Sandy leaned against the wall for support and tucked a few fallen strands of hair behind her ear. "How old is your daughter?"

"She turns five tomorrow." Holly wanted to add

that she wasn't sure how many birthdays they would get to spend together, but let that thought go unsaid. She wasn't going to add to the woman's troubles. Grace was in remission. Holly had to keep thinking positive. Still, regression was always a possibility, thus the reason she refused to stay the night. All the support groups stressed never to take a single moment for granted. They also said you had to take care of yourself too and probably would not consider driving home in a blizzard a smart thing, but Holly had her priorities. Being there for Grace was at the top of that list.

Sandy rested a hand on Holly's shoulder, blinking back tears. "You cherish every moment you have with your little girl. They grow up so quickly, and then they don't need you anymore."

For an instant, Holly thought the woman had read her mind, but one look in Sandy's eyes let her know she was referring to her own daughter. The one she thought lost to her now that she'd found someone else to take care of her. An odd feeling of kinship washed over her. They were both trying to hang on to their little girls. She took Sandy's hand and gave it a gentle squeeze. "She's just distracted at the moment. Take it from me; we always need our mamas."

The overhead lights flickered another warning. Sandy pushed off the wall and rose from her melancholy, like a benched player being pulled back into the game. "If you are not going to stay, then you'd better get going. Did my husband pay you?"

"He did." *And then some,* she thought, referring to the generous tip he'd given her.

"Good. Now get going before someone else decides to call you back for another picture," Sandy said firmly.

Holly didn't have to be told twice. She hurried into her coat and slipped out the same door the love-struck couple had used only twenty minutes before. A blast of arctic air sent snow flying into her face. All of a sudden, she was regretting the MacGyver'd use of her hat. Oh well, at least the camera was warm. She hurried to her car, head lowered against the brutal northern wind. Winter in Pennsylvania could be treacherous at times.

This was one of those times.

She hadn't expected to be leaving so late. After seeing the weather reports, she thought the party would have ended earlier than it did. She could have left sooner; the family would have understood, but she had a reputation to protect. Staying until the end was the package they'd paid for. It was expected of her, and it wasn't like the couple had planned to get married in a blinding snowstorm. The wedding had been on her books for nearly a year. It was one of the hazards of accepting a wedding gig in late January, one she'd agreed on, even knowing she would have a half-hour's drive home. "Yeah, right," she mumbled against the wind. She'd be lucky to get home at all in these conditions. She lost her footing, slipping, but managed to lift the camera case high before she hit the pavement. Fortunately, the blanket of snow helped to cushion her fall. She pushed from the fluff, managing to right herself, all while keeping the camera equipment tucked close to her body. She was not about to sacrifice hours' worth of work, especially since the bride's father had tipped her so generously for showing up in such deplorable conditions. Of course she'd showed up; she was a professional. *Neither rain, nor wind, nor sleet, nor snow. So what if that was the United States Postal Service's motto. If it worked for her father, it worked for her.* Besides, she was driving her father's Jeep, and it had seen its share of snowstorms.

Reaching the Jeep, she tugged the door against the wind, barely making it inside without falling a second time. *Maybe I should have accepted Sandy's offer.* While the smart thing, her heart pulled her in the other direction. She was going home, keeping the promise she'd made to her daughter. She waited for the engine to warm, thankful she'd raised the wiper blades upon arriving. At least they would not be stuck to the windows. As the snow started to slide down the windshield, she took off her heels and pulled on sweatpants, wool socks, and boots. No easy task while she was sitting in the driver's seat, but she managed. She wasn't making much of a fashion statement with her navy blue dress, but she was heading straight home. It wasn't like anyone would see her.

She grimaced, realizing she'd forgotten to lower the wiper blades. The wind caught the door as she opened it, flying out of her hand with enough force she was afraid it would be pulled from its hinges. Grabbing hold of the edge, she pushed it shut, hurried to scrape the remaining snow off the windshield, lowered the blades, and returned to the car, stamping the snow from her feet. She warmed her hands, cursing the fact that she'd left her gloves on the seat instead of placing them on her hands. *Oh well, at least they are still dry*, she thought, slipping them on. She considered calling her dad to let him know she was on her way, then reconsidered. If he were still awake, he would have called. No sense interrupting perfectly good sleep just to say she was okay. She placed the phone in the cup holder and placed the car in gear.

"God, please watch over me and guide me home safely," she repeated as she made her way out of the church parking lot.

Chapter Five

Having made several passes along the stretch of Route 30 to the county line, Officer Jerry McNeal was now idling in the snow-covered parking lot of Greenwood Hills Chapel. He felt certain he was close to where he would be needed and although not ready to radio for reinforcements, he knew the time was getting near. On an ordinary day – if there were such a thing when dealing with that feeling – Jerry would have asked for backup or had stations on standby, but this was no ordinary day. The roads were treacherous, the snow falling so quickly even the snowplows were having trouble keeping up. He watched the computer monitor in his patrol car scroll the latest weather advisory, which now predicted over twenty-four inches of snow by the time the system moved out. He locked his fingers together in a meditative state, extended his two index fingers, and tapped them against his mouth, watching the snow fall against the windshield. The wet flakes would barely settle before being tossed forcefully aside by the wiper blades. Out of the corner of his left eye, he saw the flashing yellow lights of a snowplow hulking its way through the intersection where 997 met Route 30. Heading east on Route 30, the blade skimmed the road, tilted slightly, shooting everything in its path to the right shoulder of the road. A shiver traveled the length of him as the truck disappeared behind a whiteout of snow, then reappeared a short time later. "God in Heaven, please watch over us all," Jerry said as the truck passed in a spray of snow followed by a beacon of yellow lights. Lights that could not be seen only seconds earlier. He felt hot air brush against the back of his neck and instantly pressed his hand to the area in question. He had a sudden feeling that he wasn't alone, yet when he looked in the mirror, he saw nothing but darkness amongst the faint glow of his parking lights reflecting in the snow.

His cell phone rang, startling him. "McNeal," he said, tearing his gaze away from the mirror.

"How's things looking out there, Jerry?" the sergeant asked.

"A little freaky."

"Say again?"

"Whiteouts so bad you can't see. I just watched an entire snowplow disappear right before my very eyes," Jerry said, checking the mirror once more.

"And the civilian traffic?"

"I wish I could say nonexistent," Jerry said, watching a late model pickup truck drive past much faster than was safe, considering the current road conditions. He considered citing the driver, but his feeling told him he was needed elsewhere.

"When they have an accident, you can bet your ass they'll blame the road commission for not having the roads cleared. How about you? That radar of yours picking up anything?"

Jerry knew his sergeant was not referring to his police radar. Not the one in his vehicle anyway. "Yeah, I think it's about that time. I don't know what yet, but pretty close to the county line on 30."

"Need me to send backup?"

"I wish I knew," Jerry said with a sigh. "I just can't see bringing everyone out in these conditions when I don't have a clue what I'm dealing with. I think I'm going to take another pass down that way. I got a really bad feeling when that snowplow went past a few moments ago."

"You do that. I'll have a couple of the boys start heading in your direction," the sergeant said.

"Okay, but tell them to take their time. I'll be back in touch as soon as I know something."

"Roger that."

Jerry switched off his phone and checked the rearview mirror one last time. He wasn't sure which was stronger, the feeling that something was going to happen or the feeling that he was no longer alone in the SUV.

***

Conditions were deteriorating at an alarming rate as Dennis made his fifth pass down Route 30. Thankfully, it seemed most were heeding the warnings, with only a few exceptions. He passed Wal-Mart, which remained open despite the conditions. He pulled into the Lowe's parking lot and let the engine idle while he unzipped his lunchbox. He opened the baggie, pulled out his turkey sandwich, peeling the bread back with the tip of his index finger, and sighed. He was glad his truck was facing west; had he turned the other direction, he would be able to see both the Wendy's and Arby's signs. Not that either was open, but that wasn't the point. He took a bite, felt the crunch of the lettuce followed by the tangy bite of yellow mustard, and chewed halfheartedly. *Boring.* That was the only way to describe it. He ate another bite, wishing he had some chips to go with it. He thought about returning to Wal-Mart. No, he couldn't do that, as technically, he was still on lunch. And he'd promised to eat only what Selina had fixed him for lunch. But if he were to stop at Rutter's during his next pass, he would be able to get something he could sink his teeth into and eat it with a clear conscience. If Selina asked if he had only eaten what she'd packed him for lunch, he could, with a clear conscience, say yes. He would just refrain from telling her about anything he'd eaten afterward. He finished eating his sandwich, which seemed to taste a bit better now that he'd worked out a plan. Next, he dove into the veggies, dipping each stick into the hummus before popping them into his mouth and crunching them into oblivion. When he finished, he ran his index finger around the container, licking the remnants from the digit before covering the container and returning it to the lunchbox. He smiled as he picked up the container that held the angel food cake. Only then did he see the note. Sitting the container in his lap, he unfolded the note.

My darling Dennis, I'm so proud of you for sticking to your diet. I know how hard it is for you, but I thank you for making this commitment to your health. The boys and I need you and would be so lost without you. You can do this. You are stronger than any craving. Please remember this anytime you get weak.

I'll reward you later,
Selina.

Dennis sighed. Lina knew him too well. Of course she'd known what he was planning. A plan he could no longer follow through with. He opened the container, removed the slice of cake, and took a small bite, chewing it slowly in an effort to make it last. He finished the cake, plucked a couple of crumbs from his shirt, and ate those as well. Halfheartedly, he closed the lid to his lunchbox. While he was no longer hungry, his tummy still wasn't quite satisfied. It was going to be a long night. He made a right turn out of the parking lot, lowering his blade as he rounded the corner, leaving a trail of dirty white in his path. Just as he passed Norlo Park, he went through a whiteout that lasted several moments. He'd driven through several more by the time he'd reached Highway 997. He caught the red light at Rutter's and shook his head. Fate was tempting him. He eased his grip on the steering wheel, only then realizing how hard he'd been gripping the wheel. He didn't mind driving in the snow. Driving blind in the midst of whiteouts was another thing altogether. If he could not see the road, chances were others on the road could not see him. At least he had the added security of the flashing lights. His security blanket vanished when a wall of white suddenly blocked his view of the red traffic light he'd seen just seconds before. The veil of snow lifted just seconds before the light switched to green.

Gripping the steering wheel, he continued on his way. He passed by Rutter's and averted his eyes to avoid further temptation. He noticed a State Trooper idling in the parking lot of Greenwood Hills Chapel and chuckled. If anyone was speeding on these roads, they deserved to be pulled over. Probably didn't even have his radar on. Taking a nap or watching a movie on his phone. *Porn.* That thought evoked another chuckle. Dark parking lot, not many people on the roads. *Yes, most definitely porn. Must be nice, being a cop. I could be a cop. I could watch porn in a snow-covered parking lot. It would beat the hell out of driving in blinding snowstorms. But hey, not everyone can be Superman.*

***

The roads were worse than Holly had imagined. A part of her wished she'd taken Sandy up on her offer to stay. A moot point now that she'd already driven far enough that turning around would defeat the point. The snow would be the same in both directions, so she might as well keep going. She saw a billboard touting Mr. Ed's Elephant Museum, one of the local touristy places. The museum housed glass cases full of elephant figurines and memorabilia and nearly as much selection when it came to candy, nuts, and fudge, which could be purchased by the piece or pound. Her mouth watered at the thought of cinnamon-flavored almonds, which were her personal favorite. She smiled, remembering the childish excitement on Grace's steroid-bloated face when she'd run through the store filling her little tin bucket with candy. How she'd stood outside bald as a billiard ball answering Miss Ellie, the talking elephant statue that was on guard near the road at the museum's entrance.

That was two years ago, when Grace first started undergoing chemo. Two long years. Grace's hair still hadn't returned, but the child always insisted Holly blow the horn every time they drove past so Miss Ellie would know they were thinking of her. Her mind drifted to her daughter, who'd been in remission for half a year. The doctors called this a positive sign, but others who'd been through the same ordeal warned her to be diligent of any signs and symptoms. Always one to think positive, Holly had not allowed such thoughts to dictate her life, still working and accepting jobs. She had bills to pay after all – but she refused to miss any important events in her daughter's life, including Grace's fifth birthday tomorrow – today, actually, as it was well past midnight.

She passed the store with the concrete monuments, gasping when the building disappeared in a haze of white before her eyes. She focused her attention back on driving, sat taller in the seat, and strained to see the road. While the roads had been plowed, the snow was still plenty deep and conditions slippery. She nearly lost control of the Jeep as she passed Cashtown Road. Such a drastic change from when she'd shot a wedding at the historic Round Barn in August. That had been a hot summer afternoon, so hot she could almost feel the warmth of the afternoon sun just thinking about it. Almost but not quite. As it was, the heater in the Jeep struggled to keep up against the wind outside, making her grateful she'd had the forethought to pull on her sweats and boots before heading out.

As she drove down the hill, she passed a snow-covered elephant on the right that announced the beginning of the elephant museum property. Just past the trees would be the museum and the famous Miss Ellie. Holly smiled, wondering if anyone would notice if she parked alongside Miss Ellie and spent the night, then, realizing she'd run out of gas before daybreak, opted to toot the horn instead. "Hi, Miss Ellie," she shouted as she drove past, then made a mental note to take Grace back to the museum once the weather cleared. It would be worth the sugar high just to have new memories of the place.

As she continued west on Route 30, the snow intensified. Whiteouts were becoming commonplace. Thankfully, she had only met three vehicles in the last ten minutes, and none appeared to be traveling in the same direction as she. The road began to level out; she could just make out the yellow flashing lights alerting her of the traffic light.

She was almost home.

Just a few more miles, and she'd be able to tiptoe into Grace's room to check on her before jumping into a warm shower to thaw out. She gripped the wheel tighter as another whiteout blocked her vision. As the snow shower cleared, she could see the yellow flashing lights looming closer. *Weren't they supposed to be higher? When had they added more lights? Why hadn't she noticed the second set of lights on her way out of town?* She squinted through the snow, trying to figure out what she was seeing before her mind registered she was heading straight into the path of a snowplow. Screaming, she whipped the steering wheel to the left, sending the Jeep fishtailing out of control. Barely missing the guardrail, she careened down the embankment and headlong into a stand of trees.

Chapter Six

Jerry crept his way along the snow-covered road, the feeling of urgency escalating with every turn of the wheel. He knew it was nearing the time when he would be needed. He traveled at what seemed a snail's pace, reminding himself he would be of no help if he ended up in a ditch. An image of the snowplow entered his mind, but something else nagged at the recesses. Something he'd yet to put his finger on. Even though the plow had passed by only moments before, the roads were so thick with freshly fallen snow that the large truck's tire tracks were already covered with snow. It didn't help that the wind was blowing so fiercely that he was driving blind most of the time, whiteouts sending veils of snow to obscure his view. A seasoned driver, he knew the truck could be right in front of him, and he wouldn't see it until it was too late. The windy road proved tricky, but he was able to stay in his lane. The snow blind lifted, the yellow caution lights dancing into view, warning of the traffic light at Route 233. Just past that would be Caledonia State Park, then the Franklin/Adams county line. A county snowplow would have to turn around soon. Jerry guessed the best spot for this was just across the county line at the Adams County fill site. The truck would have to cross traffic but could make a right turn when exiting the parking lot. The light turned red as he was approaching. Jerry looked to make certain the path was clear before proceeding through the intersection without stopping.

Just as he cleared the light, he saw what he was looking for; the large snowplow had careened into the hill on the opposite side of the road. It looked as if the blade of the plow had dug into the hillside so hard that it had slung the truck to the side, lifting the whole right side of the truck completely off the road. The truck was left teetering on the left wheels, held precariously in that position by the blade, which was embedded in the snow-covered hill. *How in the hell did he manage that?* Jerry wondered. The yellow lights on the truck were still flashing, which would hopefully keep the truck visible to oncoming traffic. Just in case, Jerry parked his SUV in the center of the road and hit the switches to every light available to him. The snow lit up in a brilliant array of blues, reds, and whites. He turned on the siren, hoping that what could not be seen could at least be heard. The wail of the siren bounced off the snow, wound down, then increased once again, echoing off the hillside. Annoying but effective, especially when conditions were at their worst.

He used his spotlight to survey the area. Not seeing anything else out of the norm, he keyed the radio, alerting dispatch. "Dispatch, this is unit 7. I've got a single vehicle accident located on Route 997 just east of the Adams County line, approximately a quarter mile past Route 233. Clear." For the sake of the driver's privacy, Jerry used the SUV's in-unit computer, quickly typing a message to dispatch, letting them know the vehicle involved was a county snowplow, asking for a large tow truck and other equipment needed to handle the scene.

"Clear, unit 7; other units are being dispatched. Please be advised due to weather conditions, response time will be hindered. Clear?"

"Clear." Jerry zipped his coat to his chin, pulling on his gloves before climbing out of his vehicle. He started towards the truck, then returned to the SUV for a first aid kit, feeling sure he'd need it. He checked under the seat, then opened the back door. The wind caught the door, whisking it from his grasp. He could have sworn he felt a rush of warm air sail past him. Not possible on a night like this, but eerie all the same. He looked around, half expecting to see someone standing behind him. No one was there. *Get a grip, Jerry.* He shrugged off the feeling of unease, found the first aid kit, and hurried to the truck. His boots sank into the depths of snow as he cautiously approached the left side of the cab. Studying the wreckage to make sure there was no chance of the truck rolling further, he squeezed his way between the truck and the hill. He tried the door, but it was locked. Not that he'd be able to open it, as there was barely enough room for him to squeeze between the truck and the hill. The windows were covered with snow; there didn't appear to be any movement within the cab. He reached for his flashlight, brushed the snow away from the side window, and illuminated the inside.

The driver was still fastened in his seat-belt, the only thing keeping the large man in his seat. Jerry was impressed the belt had held, considering the man's weight. The driver's head was hanging limp, double chin resting high on the man's chest. Jerry shouted to be heard above the siren. This did not evoke a response. He could see blood coming from the left side of the man's head. *He must have hit his head on the side window.* Jerry tapped at the window with his flashlight. Still, the man did not move. *Come on, fella, don't be dead.* Jerry pulled his cell phone out of his pocket, opting for discretion, knowing there was a good possibility the man's wife owned a police scanner. He found the number he was looking for and pressed send. "Sergeant, I need a name for the county snowplow driver running 997. Also, please verify there is an ambulance en route to this location."

"I'll get dispatch working on the name. The ambulance has been dispatched, but road conditions are keeping them from responding at present."

Jerry could hear the helplessness in the sergeant's voice, which matched the panic he was starting to feel. Something nudging at him was telling him to hurry. *Give me a break already. Can't you see I'm trying?*

"I don't care if they have to use a dog sled, get them en route," Jerry said heatedly.

"Roger. And, McNeal, we are doing the best we can. Clear?"

"Clear," Jerry said, keeping his anger in check. He was angrier at himself than at the sergeant. *If he'd only gone with his instincts and asked for backup earlier.* He tapped on the window once more and was relieved when he saw the man's eyes flicker in response. *Unconscious, not dead. Thank you, Jesus.* He tugged at the driver's side door again to no avail. Swallowing, he knew the only way in would be the passenger's side door, which meant he'd have to climb his way inside. First, he trudged his way around to the front of the truck. He aimed the beam of light at the blade, which still appeared to be firmly embedded in the hillside. He climbed onto the blade, then, using the snow-covered hillside as leverage, tried to dislodge the blade. He slipped but managed to leap clear of the blade. He was somewhat satisfied that the truck wasn't going anywhere. At least, he hoped so. *Wouldn't be much help if I were under a truck.* The siren was still wailing. He considered turning it off, but decided he'd rather put up with a bit of noise than to have someone plow into the underside of the truck. As the siren lessened, he heard a howl in the distance. He froze, listening. It too seemed to be echoing off the hillside. There were a few homes in the area, but this stretch was mostly forest. *Could be a wolf or coyote, most likely something less sinister. Probably just a family dog from one of the neighboring houses. Poor devil is probably half frozen and upset by the sirens.*

Can't say as I blame you, pal. If I had time, I'd find your owners and have a talk with them about leaving you outside on a night like this. He turned his attention back to the situation at hand. He went back to the driver's side window, pounding on the glass. "Driver, can you hear me?"

No response.

His instincts shouted to break the window so that he could get to the man, but given the man's size, there was no way Jerry would be able to pull him through the narrow opening. No, all it would do would be to further expose the man to the elements. That the man was not wearing his coat would not help his situation. Given no other choice, Jerry gripped the doorframe and began his slippery ascent up the side of the truck.

Chapter Seven

The blinking lights, the snow clearing to reveal the enormous snowplow headed straight for her; it all happened so quickly that all Holly could do was scream. She applied the brakes, but it didn't seem to help as the Jeep careened out of control. Just missing the guardrail, she felt the Jeep take flight, leaving the road, and sailing over the bed of snow. *Oh God, please don't let me die!* Limbs crashed against the Jeep as it floated down the ravine. She heard something hit the door as the Jeep passed a stand of young saplings. The Jeep headed straight towards a thicket of large, established trees. *No! No! Please no*! She made a fruitless attempt at turning the wheel, then braced for impact. She hit hard, a spray of snow billowing out in all directions. Something crashed through the windshield, plummeting to the seat beside her. She felt the Jeep buckle as it hit a sturdy tree. At the same instant, a searing pain shot through her right leg, traveling all the way up her thigh. She screamed as the airbag deployed, crashing into her so hard it stifled her scream, knocking the air out of her lungs and forcing her backward into the seat.

And then it was over.

The airbag deflated, releasing the pressure on her chest. *Am I dead?* she wondered. *Probably not, considering how bad my leg hurts.* She was trembling but had not lost consciousness. Holly took inventory. Her face hurt, but she was pretty sure the blood she tasted was from a busted lip. Her leg hurt something fierce and felt as if it was jammed into the floorboard. She tried to move it. *Holy crap!* It felt as if her leg was on fire, a searing pain that traveled all the way to her hip. Tears streamed down her face, threatening to freeze where they fell. She held her breath, clenching her teeth through the pain, and tried to pull her leg free. *Oh God!* Her breath was coming in tiny gasps as she pulled yet again, the pain racing through her like hot embers traveling the length of her torso. Still, the leg wouldn't budge. She reached for her phone, but it was not where she'd left it. She leaned forward in an attempt at finding it; her leg screamed its displeasure. She sat back in her seat, her teeth biting her lower lip as she waited for the pain to ease. She was not getting out of the car, at least not without assistance. *Is the other driver okay? Maybe he's already called for help. But what if he didn't? I'll freeze to death.*

Heavy wet snow streamed in through the broken windshield, pushed forward by the brutal force of the wind blowing into the Jeep. It was too dark to tell just how bad her situation really was. She would need to get help soon or would likely die out here. An image of Gracie came to mind. *I will not leave you, Gracie. At least not without a fight.* Holly pushed at the airbag until she could get a firm grip on the steering wheel. She held fast to the wheel as she made another attempt to pull her leg free, screaming as the Jeep played tug-o-war with her trapped limb. It was no use; the vehicle was not letting go. *Now what?* The truck driver would call for help and tell them her location. *If he were okay, he would have been down to check on me by now.* The thought chilled her further.

"Hello...HELP!" she called louder. The only sound was the wind and the occasional tree branch cracking under the weight of the snow. She brushed at the icy snow that pelted her face. *Think, Holly.* She reached into the side pocket of the door and felt something hard. Stretching her fingers further, she gripped what felt to be a flashlight. Pulling it free, she clicked the button, breathing a sigh of relief when it illuminated the inside of the cab. The relief was short-lived when she saw the condition of the Jeep. She took a breath and took stock of her situation. The window had shattered into a spider web but was intact except for a hole the size of a large beach ball where snow now streamed through. She turned the beam on the seat. A branch, which looked more like a large boulder, rested in the passenger seat. *That would have killed me if it had hit on my side.* She felt her body tremble and knew it was from more than the cold. The front end was caved around a rather large tree, her leg pinned within the wreckage. She wasn't going anywhere anytime soon. *Then I need to make sure I'm still alive when someone finally comes for me.* She shined the light in the compartment where she'd found the flashlight and saw an umbrella. Leaning to the left as carefully as she could, without moving the bottom half of her body, she reached for it, pulling it free with the tips of her fingers. She placed the flashlight into the cup holder, removed the shield from the umbrella, and held it to the side, flinching as it sprang to life. Maneuvering the umbrella, she pushed it towards the shattered windshield, the pain clawing up her leg like burning rods with each movement. After several attempts, she was able to position the umbrella in front of the windshield to offer some protection.

She sat back, brushed newly fallen tears from her face, and admired her handiwork. *Good job, MacGyver! What else you got?* she thought as she looked around the dimly lit compartment. Her gaze stopped at the camera bag. *Little good that will do me.* The bag was still in the passenger seat where she'd left it. Unfortunately, the limb that had broken the window was resting on top of it. Extending her right arm, she pulled at the log. When that didn't work, she grabbed hold of the camera bag and began to tug, straining against her injured leg. Releasing the bag, her hands flew to her leg, rubbing against the pain. Gathering her courage, she gripped the bag, tugging with all her might until, at last, she pulled the bag free. Her fingers trembled from cold and pain as she unzipped the bag. Opening the flap, Holly smiled. She'd completely forgot that she put her scarf inside when entering the church earlier that evening. She pulled out the red silk scarf, which was more for style than function. Still, it was better than nothing. She unrolled it and wrapped it around her head several times, covering her cheeks, mouth, and neck. It helped, at least a little. *How long does it take for hypothermia to kick in?* she wondered.

She removed the camera, checking for damage, and found none. Removing the lens cover, she turned on the flash and snapped a few photos of the dashboard resting on her leg, the umbrella, and the log. She lifted the umbrella, holding tight as the wind tried to blow it out of her hand, and blindly snapped several shots of the mangled car nestled against the snow-covered tree. Surely photos from the victim's point of view would be worth something. *If... she lived to share them. If not, at least Gracie would know she had been lucid enough to take photos before she died.* The thought of her daughter brought forth a new round of tears. *What would she think when her momma failed to come home?* Would she think she'd broken her promise? Or would she grow up feeling guilty, thinking it her fault that her mom had been killed? That if she hadn't made the promise to return, she wouldn't have been in the snow. *It's not your fault, baby.* Holly's feeling of helplessness was replaced with a renewed sense of determination. She returned the camera to the bag and began rubbing her gloved hands along her arms to keep the circulation flowing.

Her cell phone rang, causing her to jump, the movement leaving her gasping in pain. The floorboard on the passenger side lit up, showcasing the phone's whereabouts. The ringtone – ACDC's "Hells Bells" – let her know her dad had woken and was worried about her. "I'm not okay, send help," she called as the melody kept playing. The music stopped. Several seconds of silence passed before she heard the chime letting her know she had a new voicemail. Regret engulfed her as she recalled her decision not to text to let him know she was on her way. He would probably think she was still working. Or worse, that she'd decided to spend the night. *Note to self, if you get out of this, come up with a better plan of action for future situations such as this.* "Yeah, like not driving in blizzards," she said through chattering teeth. *God, I'm cold.*

An image of Dory – the blue and yellow fish from the Disney movie *Finding Nemo* – came to mind. "Just keep swimming, just keep swimming," the fish had repeated. "Just keep moving. Just keep moving," she said, rubbing her arms. She was still chattering the words when she heard it. A siren wailing from the top of the ridge. The sound echoing off the surrounding mountains. Rising and falling like treacherous ocean waves. Ominous on any other occasion. Tonight, the most wonderful sound she'd ever heard. *Help was coming! The snowplow driver must have called for help. He would tell them she was in the ravine and someone would come for her.*

"I'm down here!" she said, pulling the fabric

away from her mouth.

She waited for a reply. And waited. "Hello, it's pretty dang cold down here." All she could hear was the sound of the siren echoing off the rise of the hill. *Good thing they know I'm here. They would never hear me above the sound of the siren.* She pulled the mirror from where it had landed on the dashboard, held it up to look out of the rear window. The window was covered with snow, so she tossed the mirror on the seat beside the branch.

She was trembling from her head to her toes. Well, at least the toes on her left foot. Her right leg seemed to be growing numb. At least it wasn't throbbing any longer. While a relief, it probably wasn't the best of signs. *Maybe I should move it to wake it up.* A thought she discounted when just the simple act of trying to wiggle her toes sent tears streaming down her face. *Knock off the crying before the tears freeze the scarf to your face.* She wiped her eyes with a gloved hand, stopping when she had a sudden overwhelming feeling she was no longer alone.

As the siren waned, she heard a branch snap just outside the driver's side door, confirming her suspicions. "Hello? Is anyone out there?" she asked, wishing she could power down the window. She aimed the flashlight at the window, seeing nothing but her reflection in the snow-coated glass. She turned the light towards the passenger window, which once again showed nothing but her reflection.

She tried to open the door, but it wouldn't give.

Sorry, I broke your truck, Dad. "Hello? Is anyone out there? Please, if you are there, can you get me out?" *Why wasn't anyone answering?*

She heard a thump on the hood, felt the Jeep move. Fear washed over her. *Bigfoot?* Her hands trembled as she pulled the umbrella away from the window, screaming as she saw the hulking form of a very large wolf staring in through the large hole. The animal turned its head, deep brown eyes surveying her intensely. *Not a wolf, thank God. A dog. A huge German Shepherd. A police dog?* "Good Boy." God, please let him be a good boy. *Surely I didn't survive the accident just to be eaten by a dog.* She thought about asking him if he was hungry, but since she didn't have anything to offer him, decided against it. *No use giving him any ideas.*

Snow was blowing around the dog and drifting in through the broken windshield. Holly wanted to replace the umbrella but was afraid to make any sudden movements. She thought about using the umbrella to shoo the dog away, but he didn't look like the kind of animal who would be easily shooed. He looked more like the type that would get extremely pissed off if she even tried.

"Help?" The word came out in a whisper.

In response, the dog tilted its enormous head, opened its mouth, and began to howl. The animal's cry came from deep within, as if desperate to be heard over the continuing wail of the siren.

Chapter Eight

Jerry climbed his way up the slippery truck to the passenger side door. Once there, he pushed the snow away from the window and peered inside. Just as he'd expected, the door was locked. He tapped his flashlight against the window. "Driver? Can you hear me?" *I'd be surprised if you can hear anything over that damn siren,* he thought, regretting his decision to leave it on.

He palmed his hand against the window once more. "DRIVER!" *Dammit, what's this guy's name?*

Jerry's phone rang. "Talk to me," he said, forgoing the formalities.

"The driver's name is Dennis Young," the sergeant said into the phone. "Is he alive?"

"I think so. He's unconscious; I'm trying to get to him now. How about some help with that?" he added a bit more tersely.

"Take it easy, McNeal. Don't let this get personal. We both know he'd be much worse off if you'd not been called into action by that gift of yours. You know the weather conditions. Just hold on until we get there."

Holding on was precisely what he was doing,

squatting on the side of a truck held in place by the blade bolted to the front. The wind and weight of the snow that was quickly piling up on the side of the truck didn't help. Jerry was afraid it wouldn't take much for the blade to become dislodged and knew the situation could go from bad to worse at any moment. "Roger that," he said, ending the call. It was his fault. He'd known the proximity even before finding the wreckage. *Yes, but he hadn't actually known how serious the situation was going to be. Let's just hope my caution doesn't cost the man his life.*

Jerry tapped the window once more. He hesitated until the siren eased, then called to the driver, "Dennis? DENNIS! WAKE UP!" he shouted and nearly slipped off the truck when Dennis opened his eyes, lifted his head, and looked at him, blinking as if trying to focus. He watched in horror as the man's left hand went in search of the seatbelt release.

"NO!" Jerry shouted, knocking the flashlight against the glass. "Don't release that buckle!" The seatbelt was the only thing holding the man in place. Jerry was afraid that by releasing the belt, the man's weight could be the catalyst that dislodged the plow blade, the only thing keeping the truck from landing on its side.

Dennis turned his head in Jerry's direction. His brows knit together, questioning.

Jerry aimed the light into the driver's compartment. "The truck is not stable. Listen to me;

I'm a Pennsylvania State Police Officer. My name is Trooper McNeal. Whatever you do, don't release that seatbelt," Jerry shouted through the glass.

The man nodded, a movement that must have caused considerable pain as his hand flew to the side of his head. His eyes closed, then opened just as suddenly. A look of concern replaced the confusion as he brought the blood-covered hand to his face for further inspection. The man looked like a frightened rabbit.

A very large rabbit with dilated eyes.

Jerry was going to have to break the window. He took out his nightstick. "Dennis, listen to me. I'm going to help you. But to do that, I will need to break the window. Your coat is near your lap. Put your hands down, and you'll be able to feel it."

Jerry watched as Dennis' right hand found the heavy coat. "Okay, put it over your head to protect you from the glass. It's going to shatter, but it shouldn't cut you. Understand?"

Wordlessly, Dennis did as Jerry had told him.

It took two tries to break the glass. When it finally let go, it shattered into thousands of tiny, non-threatening pellets. When the spray finished, Dennis slowly lowered the coat. "I don't think the boss is going to be very happy about this." And with that, he turned his head to the left, vomiting all over the driver's side window.

Buddy, that window is the least of your worries, Jerry thought, recognizing the symptoms of a traumatic brain injury. The fact that Dennis had never once mentioned being cold also raised concerns. Jerry himself felt as though his teeth were going to shatter from chattering together.

"Dennis, I'm going to lower down into the truck with you. Okay?" Without waiting for an answer, Jerry slid the flashlight into his pocket, keeping it on so that it helped to illuminate his way. Grabbing hold of the windowsill, he lowered himself in feet first until he was somewhat sitting in the seat beside Dennis. He removed the flashlight from his pocket and positioned it so that it would light the cab but leave his hands free to attend to the driver. The stench of vomit inside the truck was overwhelming. Jerry felt his own stomach flip as the smell permeated his nostrils. *Breathe through your mouth, or you're going to lose it.* He opened his mouth slightly, then unwrapped the emergency blanket. Using the sun visor and door frame, he managed to drape the blanket enough to create a makeshift tent to protect them both from the wind and snow. Not perfect by any means, but it should hold until help arrived.

Opening the first aid kit, he fumbled for the gauze, opened the package, and placed it alongside Dennis' head. As soon as he applied pressure to the wound, Dennis jumped as if just realizing someone was with him. "Easy, big guy, it's just me, Trooper McNeal," Jerry said softly.

"The cop from outside," Dennis said, sounding groggy.

"That's right, the cop from outside," Jerry

repeated. *Keep him talking, Jerry.* "You had an accident. Do you remember what happened?"

"What happened?"

Jerry continued to apply pressure to the wound with one hand and shook the glass from Dennis' coat with the other. "That's what I'm asking you, Dennis. Do you remember what happened?" he said, tucking the coat around the man.

"A bright light," Dennis said.

Jerry caught his breath. *Had he missed something?* Another vehicle perhaps. "What kind of light, Dennis?"

"There's a cop with a bright light banging on the window."

Jerry relaxed. "That was me, Dennis; I was the one knocking on the window."

"Can you tell the cop to turn off the siren? It's hurting my head."

"I can't turn off the siren. I'm here with you. How long have you been driving the truck, Dennis?"

"I'm not driving it."

Where the hell was everyone? "Are you married, Dennis?"

"Yes."

A glimmer of hope. "What's your wife's name, Dennis?"

"Selina." The edges of his mouth turned up. "She's my angel." Even dazed, there was no doubt the man loved his wife.

"Selina, that's a beautiful name," Jerry said, still holding pressure to Dennis' head.

"She's my angel," Dennis repeated, closing his eyes.

Don't go to sleep on me. "Tell me about Selina," Jerry said, raising his voice.

"She's my beautiful firecracker with smoldering brown eyes. She's a good wife. She takes care of me." A tear trickled down his cheek. "She's the center of my world, and I don't know what my life would have been like without her."

Okay, time to change the subject. Crying was not going to solve anything. "Got any kids, Dennis?"

"I got..." Dennis stopped in midsentence. "Do you hear that?"

Actually, for the first time in nearly thirty minutes, he could hear. *Someone had turned off the siren.* He rather hoped that someone was the help they'd been waiting on.

"McNeal!?"

Thank God! "In here, Sergeant."

Jerry nearly jumped out of his skin several seconds later when a face appeared in the driver's side window.

"How are you doing in there, McNeal?" he asked, shining a light through the glass.

Freezing my nuts off.

"We're doing good. We'd be a bit better if you'd turn off your light." The light was a heavy-duty mag light and bright even to him. "Dennis here has a bit of a bump on his head. He's grateful you turned off the siren."

"Him and half the county. We've had over a

dozen complaints. Between the siren and the dog howling."

As if on cue, a howl pierced the air.

"Maybe people shouldn't leave their dogs out in this weather in the first place," Jerry answered heatedly. Jerry had a soft spot for animals, as they seemed to share the same gift as he. A knack for knowing when something was going to happen. A feeling that strangely had not lessened since he'd arrived on the scene, which was precisely why he'd left the siren on in the first place. He had a strong feeling that the worst was yet to come.

"Yes, while I'm sure most of the callers would agree with you, the rest would still like to get their beauty sleep."

"As much as I'd like to continue the conversation, I'd much rather do it from inside a warm building. Any chance of getting us out of here anytime soon?"

"I wanna go home," Dennis said in agreement.

The only place you're going is to the hospital. "We're going to get you out of here, pal," Jerry said reassuringly.

"We have help on the scene. Since there was minimal traffic on the roads, I had them come in silent. We've had enough calls. Make any more noise than necessary, and we'd be in a hell of a pickle. All we need is rubberneckers and ambulance chasers coming to see what's going on and ending up in ditches, or worse. So what do you think the chances are that your friend here can get out the same way you got in?" Sergeant Seltzer said, looking at Jerry.

Not a chance in hell. Even without the head injury, the man's size alone would keep him from it. Jerry simply shook his head in reply.

"Didn't hurt to ask. You two hold tight. I'm going to have a chat with the rescue team to see if they've formed a plan yet."

"You go right ahead, sir. Dennis and I will be right here when you figure it out. You still with me, Dennis? Hang in there. They will have us out of here in no time," Jerry said once the sergeant had left.

In the distance, he heard a dog howl. He could hear the hum of engines just beyond the cab of the truck but didn't think that was what was causing the dog's sorrowful call. It was brutally cold out. He used his free hand to tuck the heavy coat closer to Dennis. *Please God, let this man survive, and, if you're not too busy, could you please send someone to see what's bothering that dog?*

Chapter Nine

Several moments had passed and yet no one had come to check on her. No one except the dog, which now crouched on her hood staring in at her. The dog was large-boned, brown with areas of black. His ears rose up into the night, pointed and alert. The brown on his face gave way to black markings that led to a full black mask on his face. Intense, deep-set brown eyes appeared to be sizing her up as if wondering how she would taste.

"You don't want to eat me, do you, boy? How about being a good doggy and run up the hill and drag whoever is up there down here? What do you say?"

The dog licked its lips in response.

"If you're going to eat me, could you please wait until after I'm dead? It probably won't be long now, at least I don't think so. I can't feel my leg anymore; that has to mean I'm getting close to dying right?"

The dog cocked its head as if trying to decipher her words.

"Maybe you could start with my hurt leg. Just chew it off so that I can hobble out of here before I freeze to death. I don't even care if you eat the rest of that leg. I have pretty good calves; I'm sure there is enough meat on them to fill your belly. What do you say, fellow? Want to help a desperate lady out? You get to eat, and I get to live? Sound like a workable plan to you? Huh, big boy?" *What is this? Let's Make a Deal? You're losing it, Holly.*

The dog snorted its response, pushing away the umbrella and inching its massive body in through the hole and onto the dashboard.

"Oh God! HELP! Please no, please don't eat me!" she cried, using the umbrella as a shield. The large dog wasn't deterred. It brushed its way past and continued to crawl through the window, slowly making its way into the cab of the truck.

Once inside, the animal stood with its front legs on the center console, its hind legs still awkwardly resting on the dashboard. The flashlight, resting in the cupholder between the dog's legs, shot a beam upwards, showcasing the animal's rather fierce looking fangs. She closed her eyes, bracing for the impact of the teeth. She waited for several seconds before cautiously opening one eye. The beast was hulking merely inches from her face. As she opened her eye, the dog's tongue snaked from its mouth, licking her cheek. No doubt sampling before digging in.

He licked her face once more. This time, the action included a slight wag of the tail.

"Tall, dark, and friendly huh? I'd ask you to sit, but I'm afraid that seat is taken," Holly said, looking at the limb that was still resting on the passenger's seat. "I'd gladly give you my chair, but I seem to be stuck." She tried once again to pull her leg free. Either it had gone numb or her entire body was frozen.

Undeterred, the canine finished its descent into the cab before gingerly easing between Holly and the steering wheel, stretching across her lap, and covering her with its body. She removed a glove and touched a trembling hand to his fur, surprised at how warm the animal felt despite the fact that he – at least she thought it was a he – had been outside. Now that she had a chance to look more closely, she found it funny he was not covered in snow. Stranger still, he didn't appear to have any snow on him at all. *I must be hallucinating.* This thought comforted her. If she were, in fact, hallucinating, the dog probably wasn't going to eat her. *Did she imagine the siren as well? Can someone imagine something that loud? Maybe this whole thing is a dream, and I'm really home in my bed. Yes, this is all a dream. All I have to do is close my eyes and go back to sleep,* she thought, lowering her eyelids.

An instant later, her eyes flew open as the dog once again began to howl. Not a dream at all. Cold, terrified, slightly deafened by being in such close proximity to a howling dog, and trapped beneath the weight of the animal, she had been fairly certain she was in the depths of a nightmare. At least her leg didn't hurt anymore. Surprisingly, nothing hurt. But, she was cold, so terribly cold. Snow and wind drifted in through the windshield, swirling around the umbrella, which she hadn't thought to push back into its previous position. *I should fix it.* The thought passed without her acting on it. She was so very tired. She just needed to sleep.

A warm sensation aroused her once more, blinking into awareness as the dog's tongue licked the snowy flakes from her face. *I'll need a hot shower when I get home. If I live. And if I don't, what will happen to Gracie? She'll be all alone.* Holly had been hopelessly in love with Gracie's father and thought he'd felt the same way about her. At least that was the way he acted until the day Holly had shared her wonderful news with him. News he didn't think was as wonderful as she did. He made that perfectly clear when he accused Holly of trying to trap him into marriage. Her mother had told her she was a disgrace and that the child would ruin her life as she – Holly – had ruined hers, by trapping her in her own loveless marriage. Holly felt differently and considered the child her saving grace, going so far as to name her Amy Grace. A part of her wanted to name her Amazing Grace just to spite all who said the child was not welcomed, but thankfully, Holly had come to her senses before filling out the birth certificate. Even though Gracie – as she preferred to call her – was amazing, the name was too over-the-top. Holly had told her dad of the name, and he adopted it for the pet name he often used for Gracie. Her dad, while still alive, was not in the best health. What would become of Gracie if he too were not around?

Who will take care of my little Gracie!? Just the

thought of her daughter all alone in the world brought a new onslaught of tears. As if sharing in her grief, the shepherd tilted its head in a cry of solidarity. As Holly sobbed into the animal's fur, she was not aware of idling motors coming from the rise above, nor did she realize the siren had been silenced.

Chapter Ten

Jerry sat in the SUV, sipping a welcomed cup of black coffee. He normally added a bit of cream, but tonight, just the warmth of the slightly bitter brew was enough. Every bone in his body ached. He'd spent nearly three hours in the truck with Dennis, comforting him, stanching his wound, and all the while balancing so as not to fall on the man. It had taken longer than usual to round up the equipment needed at the scene, including a tow truck large enough to handle a truck that size, and a driver that was brave enough to venture out on a night such as this. After much deliberation, it was decided that the safest way to free the driver was to move the truck while Dennis and Jerry were still inside. Risky, but less so than adding the weight of a crew large enough to handle hoisting a man Dennis' size out the passenger side door. The added weight would have most likely dislodged the blade, thus sending the truck catapulting to its side. Trying to right the truck on a good day would be a fairly lengthy and complicated task; doing so in a blizzard was unthinkable. As it was, they placed blankets and pillows between Dennis' head and the window, while Jerry braced for possible impact if anything went wrong. The tow truck was able to come in from the west side and ease the truck onto all four wheels with barely any effort, leaving everyone with a sense of relief and conviction that they'd formed the best plan. The paramedics were stabilizing Dennis for the trip to the hospital. Even though he had an obvious head injury, they were fairly certain the long-term outlook was a positive one. Even with this bit of good news, Jerry still felt as if something was off. The snow had halted at some point during the rescue. Even the wind had eased its relentless assault, yet the feeling that he'd had since long before the accident had never diminished. If anything, it had increased dramatically.

What am I missing?

He'd just started to mentally retrace his steps when a light tap startled him into the present. He lowered the window, exposing the weary face of Sergeant Seltzer. The man looked every bit as exhausted as Jerry felt and just as cold.

"You doing all right, McNeal?" he asked, the words coming out in steamed breaths.

"Doing fine," Jerry lied.

"You've had one hell of a night. Why don't you go home and take a hot shower?"

God, that sounds tempting. "Not just yet, Sergeant."

Sergeant Seltzer blew into his gloved hands. "No?"

"I'm not entirely sure, but I don't think this night is over." *Not by a long shot*, he thought but neglected to add.

Seltzer sighed. "Any idea where or when?"

Now. Here. Everywhere. Focus, Jerry, he willed silently. "I wish I knew."

"Is this the same as before? I mean, the accident scene is not even fully cleared. Maybe it's just some residual ESP or something," Seltzer offered with a nod towards the ambulance.

Jerry followed his gaze, taking in the surroundings. The road was blocked in both directions. A handful of cars idled, waiting until the path cleared. Normal procedure would be to set up a detour, but the back roads were impassable. Several firetrucks, the tow truck, two ambulances – a second rig had been requested just in case the truck had toppled with Jerry still inside. Since the second ambulance was not yet needed elsewhere, the crew remained on-site and were currently chatting with other emergency personnel. People were milling about, offering comments about what they supposed had happened, most deciding the driver had swerved to miss hitting a deer or bear – unanimously adding he should have hit the animal instead of driving into the mountain. In every way a normal post-accident scene, which projected a sense of relief that help had arrived in time. Not one to justify the hairs on the back of Jerry's neck prickling as if infested with lice. But that was exactly what it felt like, as if he were going to crawl right out of his skin.

"I hope you're right." *Not a chance in hell*. He'd never had a feeling this strong before, and he'd had some pretty big hunches to contend with. *No, this felt as if his life depended on it. Whatever "it" was.*

What am I missing? The thought hammered at him like a jackhammer surging through concrete.

"Looks like the ambulance crew is getting ready to roll. Want to go check on the patient?"

"Nah, you go on ahead. I want to stay in front of the heater a bit longer," Jerry said, powering up the window. He needed to concentrate, and he could not do that with all the pats on the back, telling him he'd done it again. Or using the "H" word. Jerry was a guy who sometimes knew things; in his mind, that did not make him a hero. He put his hands together in prayer form, resting his chin on his thumbs and pressing both index fingers against his mouth; he closed his eyes. He was not sure why this seemed to work, but often, it did.

What am I missing?

Instantly, he was back parked at the chapel, watching as the snowplow drove past. The driver had looked in his direction and smiled. *Did he see him smile or did he imagine it?* It didn't really matter. *Or did it? Had the driver planned the accident? Had he intentionally driven towards the side of the mountain, gotten cold feet at the very last second, veering so that the side of the plow was the only thing that hit? Maybe, but doubtful.* By the time Jerry had arrived, his tracks had been covered by blowing snow, so, unless the driver remembered what happened, they likely might never know.

What am I missing?

What about the theory the crew had? That he had swerved to miss hitting an animal. Unlikely. According to dispatch, the driver was seasoned; he would have known an animal wouldn't have damaged the truck. Doubtful he would chance wrecking the truck just to avoid Bambi. Unless he was an animal lover. Plausible, but Jerry didn't think so. Jerry, an animal lover himself, would have put his own safety first.

What am I missing?

Could have been another vehicle. Except for the fact that the guardrail is intact. It was; that was the first thing Jerry had observed when he'd arrived at the scene and did his initial assessment.

Once again, Jerry was lured back to the present as the ambulance door slammed, signaling they were ready to head out. *God be with you all.* He watched as they slowly drove away, lights dancing off the freshly fallen snow. Sergeant Seltzer was heading his way. Sighing, Jerry drank the last of his coffee and got out to meet the man, who looked as if he were about to drop. It had been a long night for everyone.

"How's that feeling of yours, McNeal?" he asked as he approached.

"Still there," Jerry said reluctantly. *No use sugarcoating it.*

"So what do you want to do about it? Everyone is freezing their balls off and ready to head back in."

Before Jerry could answer, a sorrowful howl echoed off the mountainside. Anger fueled his answer. "Tell them to do jumping jacks for all I care! I'm going to find that dog, and get him inside where it's warm."

Jerry knew he was out of line, but he was on edge. The feeling that he was missing something nagged at him like buzzards circling fresh roadkill on a busy highway. Relentless, but just out of grasp.

"You sure that's such a good idea? He's down in the ravine from the sound of it. That snow has got to be at least three feet deep."

"I think it's a splendid idea," Jerry said heatedly. "I'm going to find that dog, see if he's got a collar, and if he does, I'm going to shove it up his owner's ass. Maybe then he'll think twice about leaving the poor thing out on a night like this."

"Easy, Trooper," Seltzer said evenly. "I know you are off your feed but try to keep it together."

Jerry stormed past, nearly slipping as he did.

"McNeal...Jerry!" Seltzer called after him when he didn't answer.

It wasn't really about the dog. Sure he felt sorry for the beast, but he was a dog after all. It was more the act of actually doing something that Jerry needed. Something, anything that would distract him enough so that he could figure out what he was missing. As he neared the guardrail, the feeling of urgency intensified. *Was it the dog he was meant to save after all?* He pulled out his flashlight, aiming it towards the ravine. The beam shone brightly against the snow. The trees were covered in layers of brilliant white. At first, he didn't see anything.

Nothing out of the ordinary anyway. Then all the pieces of the puzzle came slamming into place, like a floodgate blocking rushing water. The beam of his flashlight had reflected off the smallest glint of metal, miraculously left uncovered from the blowing winds and out of place in a forest laced with trees. Jerry knew what it was the instant he saw it. The feeling that he was missing something lifted the second his mind embraced what he was seeing.

Another vehicle!

Chapter Eleven

"We have a second vehicle!" Jerry shouted over his shoulder. The instant the feeling of imminent doom lifted, he felt rejuvenated. He rushed down the ravine, oblivious of anything except reaching the wreckage and seeing if whoever was inside was okay. *Of course they are not okay. If they were, they would have made their way up the hill by now. At least let them be alive.* Now that the feeling had lifted, another took its place, one of regret. He should have looked closer. The beam from his flashlight wavered, then brightened once more. As it dimmed yet again, he tripped over a log and nearly plummeted into the deep snow. He'd nearly taxed the batteries while waiting with the other driver. *Slow down, Jerry. Not going to be of any help if you faceplant into a tree.* He slowed his pace, picking his way carefully down the slippery slope. His thoughts traveled to the dog. *It must have been calling for help. That dog is the real hero. If not for that animal, we would have all driven away.* He glanced over his shoulder and was relieved to see lights. Help was on its way. *Please don't let it be too late.* He took comfort in the fact that the dog had survived. *Maybe there is still hope for whoever else was in the vehicle.* Still, with the length of time that had passed, hypothermia was a given.

Jerry reached the vehicle, a smaller Jeep. *Four people at the most.* The Jeep had skimmed a tree, which appeared to be blocking the driver's door. *At least it didn't hit it head-on.* The relief was short-lived when the faded beam from his flashlight showed a much larger tree had indeed stopped the Jeep's descent, and it had hit hard enough to cave in the front of the truck. A second later, he saw the broken window on the front right side. *Had someone been ejected upon impact?* He aimed the beam to the front of the Jeep, knowing that if anyone were indeed ejected, there would not be any need to hurry. He took a breath as he rounded the Jeep, stepping as carefully as possible just in case a body lay beneath the snow. Once on the passenger side, he peered into the side window, letting out the breath only when he found the seat empty, except for a large limb that rested in the passenger seat. *Not a body, a limb. Thank you, Jesus!* He made a quick sweep of the vehicle, checking for other occupants before turning his attention to the driver. He couldn't see her face, but from the clothing – long black coat and the bright red scarf wrapped around her mouth and neck – he was fairly certain the victim was a female. "Ma'am. I'm Trooper Jerry McNeal of the Pennsylvania State Police Department. Can you hear me?"

"What took you so long?" The voice was weak but surprisingly lucid.

I'm sorry...I was stupid. I should have checked.

I knew something was wrong. I didn't see any tracks and the guardrail was intact. I should have looked closer. I trusted my eyes instead of my feeling.

"Hello? Please tell me you're not a dream."

"No, I'm not a dream. It took me longer than it should have, but I'm here now," he said, shivering against the chill. While the actual snow had stopped, the wind continued to blow, causing the snow to whirl in icy blasts. A huge branch fell, just missing him, disappearing into the snow in a puff of white. He pulled the passenger door, which was locked. "Ma'am, can you unlock the door?"

"Where did your dog go?"

My dog? She must be confused.

Jerry looked in the back seat once more. The second sweep of the interior confirmed what he'd already determined. Except for the driver, the Jeep was empty. *He must have gotten scared and ran away when he heard me coming.* "Don't worry, ma'am, we'll find *your* dog," he said, putting emphasis on the word "your." "But first, we need to get you out. Can you unlock the door?"

The woman leaned to the side, fumbled with the lock, then stopped. She closed her eyes briefly before trying again, pressing it with the bare fingers of her right hand. It was then he noticed the gloves, which rested on the center console, well within reach. *Why on earth would she have taken her gloves off? Or not put them on in the first place?* Obviously, the woman was not thinking clearly. *Yet she has enough presence of mind to do as I ask,* he thought as the latch sprang up, unlocking the door to allow him access. Opening the door, he wrapped his arms around the log and wrestled it from the seat. *She was damn lucky.* He moved the bag and slid into the seat beside her. He removed her flashlight from the cup dispenser, pushed the button, and nothing happened. *Damn! How long has this thing been dead?* He tossed the light aside, placing his dwindling light in the holder. Removing his gloves, he reached for her hands, his only thought to keep them warm until the others arrived. Her grip was amazingly warm. *How could her hands be so warm after being trapped for so long?* At first glance, there were no obvious signs of hypothermia. A miracle, considering how long she'd been exposed to the elements. He marveled at the umbrella, which was shoved into the open windshield, and admired her ingenuity. *Could that simple wind block be the reason she had not succumbed to hypothermia? Not likely. It would have helped, but it wouldn't explain how warm her hands felt.*

"Can you move?"

She shook her head in response. "My leg is trapped. It hurt at first, but I can't feel it anymore. Probably not a good sign."

Probably not. "We'll get you out of here in no time. The firemen will be here any moment." He tried to sound positive. "Ma'am, can you tell me your name?"

"Holly."

Pretty name. It reminds me of Christmas. "A

Christmas baby?" he asked, following his hunch.

"How'd… you …guess?" Her teeth were chattering. Funny, she hadn't seemed that cold when he'd arrived.

"I'm a cop, remember. It's what we do."

"You must be pretty good at your job."

If I'd been better, I'd have found you sooner. "I do my best."

"You found me, didn't you? I… thin…k that mmmakes you pretty good. I'm sooo cold."

It seemed as if she were deteriorating before his very eyes. As if she was just now feeling the cold, even though she'd been exposed to the elements for several hours. *Why now?*

Jerry rubbed her fingers between his bare hands. "You weren't cold before?"

"No, your dog kept me warm."

My dog?

He was just about to voice the question aloud when the interior of the cab lit up, announcing the rescue workers' arrival. Multiple voices could be heard just outside the window. The lights became brighter as gloved hands began clearing the snow away from the Jeep.

She turned towards him, pulled the scarf away from her mouth, and gave him a trembling smile. "Nice to finally meet you, Trooper McNeal."

"It's you!" If he hadn't already been sitting, the jolt would have sent him hurtling back. While he didn't personally know her, he'd seen this lady multiple times over the last couple of weeks. In the halls of the hospital mostly, when he'd been there visiting his elderly neighbor, who was declining in health. Once he'd almost gotten up the nerve to speak to her, almost. How could he not have recognized her? Maybe it was because of all the dark mascara that trailed down her cheeks, showing the path of her tears. *Tears because she'd been left alone in the dark for so long. I'm sorry, Holly.* He longed to wrap his arms around her, tell her she was safe, and apologize for not finding her sooner. Instead, he continued to rub her hands with his. It was enough. *For now.*

"How is the other driver?"

"He's pretty banged up, but he should make it."

"There was a horrible whiteout. I thought the light I was seeing was the caution light, but then the snow cleared, and I realized there were two sets of lights. The caution light and those from the snowplow and I was heading straight for the center of the blade. I turned the wheel and pressed on the gas, hoping to get out of the way. I think I may have been airborne when I left the road. I guess I overreacted. Oh well, at least I also missed the guardrail. Lucky me," she said through chattering teeth.

But if you'd hit the guardrail, I would have found you sooner. How many hours had the blood supply been cut off from her injured leg? "Lucky you," Jerry repeated with a gentle squeeze to her hand.

"Why, hello, young lady. It appears you might have made a wrong turn," Sergeant Seltzer said as his face appeared in front of the broken window.

Jerry watched as a calculating look crossed Holly's face. "Someone told me the snow might be good for sledding. I thought I'd check it out myself before bringing my daughter out and disappointing her."

Jerry felt an irrational twinge of jealousy at the mention of a daughter; the emotion left as quickly as it had arisen. Could it have been because, at that exact moment, his fingers were tracing the spot where a ring should have been if she'd been married? *Feeling protective over someone who needs your assistance is part of the job.*

"Is there anyone you want us to call to let know you are okay?" Seltzer asked as he handed Jerry several pouches through the open windshield.

"My dad. He's all I got. Besides my daughter, that is."

She's not married. The admission pleased him more than he could have imagined as he fumbled to open one of the pouches. "Blankets," he said as he finally ripped open the small pouch.

"What are we supposed to do with it? Piece it together ourselves?"

Pretty and quick-witted. "Don't worry; they are plenty big," he said, unraveling the silver emergency blanket. "They don't look like much, but they were designed by astronauts and do a pretty good job at holding in the heat."

He began to cover her with the blanket, tucking it in and around her to help get her warm. *If you had any to hold in,* he thought, looking at her blue-tinged lips. "Sergeant, can you see if you can get us some hot packs?"

"And coffee?" Holly asked hopefully.

"Not worried it will keep you awake?"

"It's way past my bedtime. What's a few more hours?"

"Coffee it is, then. Oh, waiter," he said the next time Seltzer stuck his head in the window, "we'd like two piping hot coffees to go."

"How about a couple of hot packs instead?" Seltzer said, handing in several more small packages.

"What is he? The small package king?" Holly quipped, then blushed when she realized what she'd said.

"I've heard rumors to that effect," Jerry said as he pushed into the plastic to activate the hot pack.

"Very funny, McNeal. Ask your wife about my package the next time you see her," Seltzer said and turned away in a huff.

"I'm sorry, I didn't mean to bring your wife into it," Holly said quietly.

Jerry laughed. "The joke's on him. I'm not married."

He watched as a smile touched her eyes. *Had she been worried that he was?*

"Well, then, nice to meet you, Trooper McNeal," Holly said and reached her hand out of the blanket.

Easy, Jerry, don't let a simple rescue turn into a date, he reminded himself. Instead of taking her exposed hand, he pushed a warm pack into her palm.

"Ooohhh, this feels so good."

"Yes, maybe you shouldn't have offended the guy. You never know what kind of goodies he might bring," Jerry said, trying to keep her mind off her situation.

"Like doughnuts?"

Jerry rolled his eyes. *If he had a nickel for every doughnut quip he'd heard since becoming a cop...*

"Sorry, I tend to make jokes when I'm nervous."

"So do I and I've not made one single joke. That should let you know everything will be just fine."

"Promise?" She looked towards her leg, which while trapped and resting at a slightly odd angle, didn't seem to be causing her any undue discomfort.

God, please don't let her lose her leg.

As if she'd heard his thoughts, she turned her head towards him, blinking at him as pools of liquid rimmed her soft doe eyes. Hopeful, yet not fully trusting as they waited for him to respond.

Don't say it, Jerry. "I promise."

Shit...

Chapter Twelve

In his line of work, he'd often said things like: *You're going to be okay. It's not as bad as it looks. It's just a flesh wound* – just to ease the situation. Until this moment, saying those things had just been part of the job. Now, as he sat next to her, he needed the words he'd said to be true. Why was it so important to him? That was the part that was unclear. Maybe it was the way she'd been looking at him when he assured her she was going to be okay. *Yeah, that had to be it.* It wasn't as if he had any actual feelings for the woman. He'd just met her after all. Sure, he'd noticed her in passing once or twice. Maybe that was why the feeling had grown so intense in the first place because he knew the person involved. Near the end, he'd felt like he was going to explode. *And why was that?* The feeling had totally engulfed him. Almost as if his life had depended on it. And then just merely finding the wreckage, the sense of dread had lifted. As if he knew at that exact point everything was going to be okay. Only it wasn't, not totally anyway. She was still trapped, and even though he wasn't a doctor, he was pretty sure the blood flow had been cut off from her leg for way too long. They sat huddled under a tarp, which had been spread inside the car, while the rescue team figured the best route to freeing Holly from the wreckage.

They had the silver blanket wrapped around them, and a fistful of charcoal-activated warming packets. All in all, they were fairly comfortable. A new flashlight lit the confines of the tarp, making it seem more like a tent and reminding him of his days as a Boy Scout camping under the stars. She'd asked him to stay with her, refusing to allow a paramedic to take his place. He would have left if asked but was grateful she had insisted he stay and would have considered this a romantic setting – if not for the dire circumstances and the questionable outcome. What if she lost her leg? *Don't go there, Jerry.*

"You are awful quiet over there," she said, pulling him away from his thoughts. "I'm not stupid."

"Excuse me?"

"I'm going to lose my right leg. You know it too; that's why you turned away as soon as you made the promise."

"I know no such thing." *Only he did, at least on some level.*

"It's okay; I figured as much when the pain went away." Her voice sounded resigned to the fact.

"We have some of the best people there are working to help you. You have to think positive." Christ, that sounded as rehearsed as when he read the Miranda rights.

She laughed.

"What's so funny?" As if he didn't know.

"I gave the same speech to my daughter when she was going through her chemo."

Cancer? That would explain why she spent so much time in the hospital. And he'd thought she worked there.

"Leukemia. She's in remission," she said before he could ask.

He could hear the team outside. They were getting ready to begin using the Jaws of Life. With luck, they'd have her out soon. "What's your daughter's name?" he asked, hoping to keep her distracted.

"Grace. I call her Gracie. It's her birthday. She's five. There were times when I wasn't sure if she would make it to her birthday, and then she started getting better." Her voice cracked. "I promised her I'd be home for it. I should have stayed the night in Gettysburg, but I promised."

Tears slipped from her eyes and began dripping onto the silver blanket. He started to wipe them from her face, then reconsidered. Better to let her worry about her daughter. Love could be a mighty big motivator. "How long has she been in remission?"

"Six months. Six wonderful, amazing months."

The tarp lifted and Seltzer poked his head in through the windshield. "How are you holding up, ma'am?"

"I'd be better if I could get out of here," Holly said, wiping at the tears.

"We are going to have you out soon. You are

going to hear a lot of popping and cracking as we cut the car away from you. Understand?"

Jerry watched as she appeared to swallow her fear. "I guess my dad's not going to be getting his Jeep back?"

"He's getting his daughter back, and I'm sure that is all that will matter to him. You let us know if you need anything." He gave Jerry a pointed look – which Jerry knew meant to keep her calm – before lowering the flap to keep the heat from escaping.

A sharp pop followed by the sound of something pelting against the tarp caused Holly to jump. He watched as her eyes flew open. She moved a hand towards the tarp.

"Leave it," he said briskly. "Sorry, it was glass from the side window. Next, they are going to be removing the door and roof." Instantly, he could hear popping and creaking as the Jaws of Life began eating away at the steel.

"Why were you in Gettysburg?" Jerry asked.

"What?" she asked absently.

"You said you should have spent the night in Gettysburg. Never mind what's going on outside. It's just you and me. Talk to me." *Please.*

"I...I was taking pictures. At a wedding. I'm a photographer."

Shit! He reached into the floor between his legs and brought up the bag he'd carelessly pushed to the side when entering. He frowned, noting the bag was slightly wet where the snow had melted from his boots. Unzipping the bag, he withdrew the camera and inspected it for any visible damage, breathing a sigh of relief when he saw it seemed to be unscathed. He was just about to return it to its case when Holly reached for it. Turning it on, she snapped a photo of him.

"You would probably do better with this," he said and handed her the flash attachment.

Holly slipped the flash into the horseshoe-shaped crease and took several more photos, the flash looking like a strobe within the confines of the tarp.

He closed his eyes, trying to get rid of the light that momentarily burned into his retinas.

She aimed the camera for yet another shot when someone on the other side of the tarp yelled for others to lift the roof from the car. "I guess things are about to get interesting," she said as she lowered the camera. "Maybe I could get them to remove the tarp so I can get some decent shots."

"You're kidding, right?"

"I took some earlier. Ya know, to document what had happened in case..." Her voice trailed off.

"In case we didn't find you in time," he said, finishing her sentence.

"It had crossed my mind at first," she admitted.

"I'm sorry I didn't find you earlier." Guilt clawed at him. He'd known something was wrong. Why the hell hadn't he listened to his feeling?

Her brows knitted together. "But you knew I was here. That's why you sent your dog."

It was the second time she'd assumed the dog to be his. *What had happened to the thing?* "My dog?"

"Yes, the police dog. He scared me at first, but then I knew you'd sent him to keep me warm. How do you train them to do that?"

Now he was even more confused. "Trained him to what?"

"To keep people warm."

"Holly, I'm afraid I don't have any idea what you are talking about. I don't have a dog."

"Well, someone sent him. One of the other officers, maybe?"

There was no one else with me. "So what makes you so sure this dog was a police dog?"

"The tag on his collar, PSPD090."

PSPD090, Pennsylvania State Police Department. A chill raced across his arms. He knew that number. Everyone in his department knew that number. They also knew the number was officially retired. K-9 090, AKA Gunter, had received a medal of commendation last week. Only he was not here to accept the award; he'd died in the line of duty days earlier when he'd leapt in front of a bullet. A bullet intended for his partner, handler Sergeant Brad Manning. Manning was still on mandatory leave. In fact, it was Manning's SUV Jerry had driven this evening. A sudden recollection of having felt he'd not been alone in the patrol unit had Jerry's heart racing. *Don't lose your head, Jerry; there has to be a logical explanation for this.* "What do you mean the dog kept you warm?" He hoped his voice sounded calmer than he felt.

"He crawled into my lap and kept licking my

face. My hands were freezing, even with my gloves on, so I got the idea to take them off and place them under the dog's fur. It worked."

That explained why she seemed to have suffered no ill effects from prolonged exposure. The dog's body heat had kept her warm. Except for the fact that a ghost dog wouldn't be warm. Would it? *Hold it together, McNeal.* "Are you sure of the tag?" *Of course she's sure. Probably read an article about the dog's heroism in the paper and had hallucinated the whole thing. Then why was she so warm?*

"Yes, I mean, I think so... There was a tag. I guess I could be wrong about the number, though."

Of course, you are. But then where did the dog come from? And more importantly, where did it go? Yeah, just the facts, ma'am. You need to take your own advice, Jerry. Like the fact that if a police dog had gotten loose from another district, then the police department would have sent out a BOLO. So why hadn't the police department sent one out? Easy, Jerry, because you can't Be On the Look Out for a dead dog.

Holly gasped, pulling him abruptly from his musings. In his peripheral vision, he saw the camera gliding to the floor, seemingly in slow motion. He reacted in time to keep the camera from hitting the floor, grasping it triumphantly between his first finger and thumb. He was just about to proclaim his heroics when Holly's screams filled the early morning air.

Chapter Thirteen

Jerry paced the halls of the emergency room at the Chambersburg Hospital, where they'd taken Holly. Normally, they would have flown her to a trauma center, but weather conditions did not allow for the helicopter to take flight. Instead, paramedics routed to the nearest hospital for stabilization. He'd followed the ambulance, just to be sure she arrived safe, then found he couldn't leave. Not without knowing she'd be okay. Her screams still haunted him. He'd been sure they'd cut her leg off when extricating her from the car, but thankfully, that had not been the case. The sudden intense pain was caused by the release of pressure. Once her leg was cut free, the nerve endings reawakened, sending pain signals to the brain. A good sign, according to the paramedics on scene.

As he started down the corridor for the umpteenth time, the lobby entrance doors at the end of the hallway slid open. An elderly man trudged into the corridor, carrying a bleary-eyed little girl. While the child was well past the age of needing carrying, he seemed in no hurry to put her down. The old man's face looked haggard under his gray bed-tossed hair. Bootlaces trailed behind, as if he'd dressed too hastily to have bothered with them.

Jerry's eyes shifted to the child, who had fared better than the man carrying her. She was wearing a bright pink coat with a matching knitted hat that covered her head. What looked to be pajama pants were tucked securely into boots, which were laced and tied at the top. Unnecessary, since by the looks of it, the child's feet had never actually touched the snow. The girl blinked against the brightness, yawned, and rubbed a tight fist against her eye. As she lowered her hand, he could see the red-rimmed lids of her eyes – eyes that looked exceedingly bright despite her puffy white face. *Is she hurt or sick?* Even as his mind registered the question, Jerry realized he had instinctively moved towards the duo. Jerry took a step closer, but before he could fully reach them, the man grabbed on to the sleeve of a passing hospital worker. *A lab tech*, Jerry noted upon seeing the plastic basket that held slender glass tubes in the worker's right hand.

"My daughter was in an accident. They told me she was in Bed Three. Can you show me where it is?" the man asked frantically.

The lab tech shifted the basket to his left hand before placing his now free hand reassuringly under the man's arm. The technician was good. Jerry held back as the tech led them over to the nurses' station. Jerry was pleased to see the worker stay with the man and child until he'd gotten the information needed. Within moments, the tech brushed past Jerry with the man and child following. The older man made eye contact with Jerry as he passed. Jerry offered a nod of encouragement and was surprised at the twinge of envy he experienced as the trio disappeared behind the curtain where they were keeping Holly. *That must have been Holly's dad and her daughter. Not sick then, not anymore.* He smiled, remembering Holly said the child was in remission. For some reason, that thought lifted his spirits. The child is a fighter. *Gracie,* he thought, remembering her name. She had to get her fighting spirit from someone. *I hope that someone is her mother.*

Jerry moved closer to the curtain, wishing he too had been allowed inside. *You're going above and beyond, Jer. Just go home and get some sleep. It's been a difficult day; you can call and check on her status in the morning.* He was tired. A hot shower and firm bed sounded exceedingly inviting. Still, he made no move to leave. He patted the pocket of his heavy winter coat, which was draped across his left arm, and started as the curtain leading to Holly's cubicle parted. The lab tech stepped out into the hall, scanned the hallway, and set off in his earlier direction. Jerry took off his hat and rubbed his free hand across his smooth head. As his hand trailed down the back of his skull, the curtain slid open. The old man walked out, followed by the little girl. She peered up at him, and for the first time, he could see her resemblance to her mother. As the man stepped around him, Jerry saw unshed tears brimming in his eyes. *Are they tears of remorse or relief?* He moved to ask the man when he felt something tug at the coat he was holding. He looked down into the worried face of Holly's daughter.

"The doctors will fix you," Gracie said in a solemn voice.

Puzzled, he knelt down to her level. "Excuse me?"

Gracie pointed to his head, then pulled off her cap to display her own hairless scalp. "I was sick too, but the doctors fixed me. They are fixing my mommy too. Mommy said they are angels; they will fix you too."

Jerry felt his eyes moisten. *She thinks I'm sick. Worried about strangers at a time like this.* "Oh, honey, I'm not sick. My hair will grow back."

"Mine too!" Gracie said before trailing her grandfather down the hall.

Jerry thought about going after her and explaining he'd shaved his head by choice but didn't want to leave Holly. He was not leaving until he knew she was going to be all right. He leaned against the wall, waiting. Suddenly, the nurse stuck her head out of the enclosure. The tall, thin woman with her hair pulled back in a no-nonsense bun, looked at him with an expression that said *I'm in charge and you'd best remember that.* "Trooper McNeal?" the woman asked upon seeing him.

He pushed off the wall. "Yes?"

She appraised him briefly, then smiled. It was a slight smile, one that he may have missed if he hadn't seen the transition. "Miss Wood is asking to see you. She said you are the one who saved her life."

"Among others."

"Yes, well, she wants to see you." She leveled a look at him, and for a second, he thought she was going to renege on her invitation. "Don't stay long; she's been through a lot this evening."

That's putting it mildly. "Yes, ma'am," Jerry said and stepped around the woman. As he passed through the opening in the curtain, he was once more surprised to find his heart rate elevated. *Get a grip, Jer. You're acting like a schoolboy.* A schoolboy who nearly leaped for joy when he saw Holly smiling up at him from her hospital bed. Her face was bruised, her nose swollen but didn't appear to be broken. Her lip was split and coated with a glistening salve. She would no doubt have double black eyes by the day's end, but all in all, Jerry thought she looked beautiful. As beautiful as someone who looked as if she'd just spent a round in a boxing ring with Mike Tyson could.

"Miss Wood, how are you feeling?" he asked in his best cop voice.

"Seriously? With everything we've been through, you can't call me by my first name?"

"How are you feeling, Holly?" he said more gently.

She lifted her arm to show him the IV. "Pretty darn good. I'm not sure what's in here, but I could have used some of this stuff earlier."

He remembered her scream. Something told him he would always remember that scream. "I thought…"

"Truth be told, so did I."

"How is it? Your leg?" he asked, nodding toward the covers. *I don't care as long as the rest of you is okay.*

"They're not sure yet, but they think I may be able to keep it. I'm not sure how it will look in a pair of shorts, but I guess we can't have everything."

"Oh thank God," he said, voicing his relief out loud.

"He had help," she said, beaming up at him. "He sent me an angel."

You may be more right than you know. An image of Gunter floated through his mind.

"You have a hard time with this whole hero thing, don't you?" she asked.

He held two fingers together near his face. "A wee bit. Besides, I think most of the credit belongs to the dog. Wouldn't you say?"

A frown replaced her smile. "Did you ever find him?"

"We did not." If he was even ever there. *You heard him yourself, Jerry.*

"But you are positive you didn't send him?"

He wanted to humor her, to tell her he'd been mistaken, that he'd watched him flee the scene, but he couldn't lie to her. "I did not."

"And no one else did?"

He shook his head.

"You don't believe me, do you?"

God help me, but I do. "I heard the dog myself.

But it would have been nice to have actually seen the thing." *Just so I could be sure...*

"Oh, that's easy." The smile returned to her face.

"It is?"

"Sure! I took a picture of him!" The smile left her face. "Please tell me my camera survived."

A picture?! He slid into the chair beside her bed, fished in his coat pocket, and withdrew the camera. "I'm afraid the bag itself didn't make it." He tugged on the coat, found the inside pocket, and withdrew the flash, which he'd dismantled. Thankfully, his service coat had deep utility pockets.

"You didn't look through the photos?" she asked, taking the camera from him.

"Of course not; that would have been an invasion of privacy, and the law frowns upon that sort of thing." What he didn't tell her was that his fingers had caressed that camera repeatedly while he'd struggled with his mind, which was trying to coax him into having just one little peek. A glimpse into a world seen through her eyes. How close he'd come to invading her privacy. How sure he'd been that if she hadn't made it, her family would never have known he'd taken the camera. It would be his link to her. To this woman who'd first captured his heart weeks ago, when he had seen her roaming the halls of this very hospital. *Oh, Jerry, they would take away your gun if they knew how bonkers you...*

"Here he is," Holly said, thrusting the camera in his direction. "See? Told you I wasn't hallucinating!"

***

He'd only gotten a brief look at the photo before the orderly had pulled back the curtain, bursting through like Jack Nicholson in the movie *The Shining* – here's Johnny! Actually, he'd said something more along the lines of *Miss Wood, my name is Donny, and I'm here to take you down to x-ray,* but it had had the same surreal feel. Especially when Jerry had just seen a photo of a dog who was supposed to be dead. He was dead, damn it; Jerry was sure of that. Jerry thought it would have been a coincidence: two shepherds with the same markings, the same torn ear – a crackhead had bitten the dog in retaliation from the dog biting him – but no sort of coincidence would account for the tag. Holly was good at her job, yes sir; not many in her situation would have thought to focus on that tag. The numbers were clear. No mistake about it, the dog in the picture was the same dog. The question now was, did he tell her? *Um, I hate to tell you this, but the dog in the photo is a ghost. Maybe you should not tell anyone because they will think you are crazy.* He would need to figure it out by the time they next spoke. And they would speak. A smile crossed his lips, remembering her last words. *You still owe me a coffee; we'll consider it our second date.* Maybe it had been the contents of the IV speaking, but he thought she sounded sincere.

"You did a fine job, McNeal," Seltzer said,

clapping him on the shoulder with a firm hand.

"Yeah, I'd have done a better one if I'd found her sooner. If only…"

The sergeant dug his fingers into Jerry's shoulder. "If only what?!"

Jerry shook his head. "I knew something wasn't right. I should have looked harder when I first arrived at the scene."

Seltzer released his grip. "Damn it, Jerry. Quit beating yourself up. If only. I have your 'if only.' If only you didn't have that wonderful gift of yours, that little lady would still be at the bottom of that ravine. Sure, someone would probably have happened along the snowplow at some point, but do you think they would have found the girl? By the time someone would have filed a missing person's report, the buzzards would have been circling overhead. The only reason she is still alive is because of you. And only you. *Comprende?*"

"I understand." *I also understand I had help out there tonight.* "Sergeant? Did anyone ever find that dog?"

With that, the man burst out laughing. "Jesus, Jerry, give it a rest. I'm sure that mutt has found its way home by now. Although come to think of it, you may owe the dog a nice juicy bone. If you hadn't been all fired up about it being left in the cold, you might not have stumbled onto the girl. I guess it's safe to say you had help with this one."

Jerry felt the tension leave his shoulders. "I'd put money on it."

Chapter Fourteen

Pennsylvania State Police Trooper Jerry McNeal slipped two fingers into the elastic waistband of his briefs, sliding them across his hips, watching as they fell without protest to the cold tiled floor. He pulled open the shower door, turned on the faucet, and stepped inside without waiting for the water to warm. He needed the shock value, which was exactly what he got. It was bitterly cold outside and the water coming in through the pipes jolted his senses in a way even a steamy cup of coffee couldn't equal. He screamed obscenities the second the icy fingers touched his skin. He pressed his hands against the wall, leaning into the spray and swearing once more as the water trailed lower down his exposed flesh. He tilted his head, closing his eyes as the stream bounced off his freshly shaved skull. He shivered as he waited for the water to warm. "Suck it up, McNeal. It's too early on a Sunday morning for you to be talking shit," he scolded. It was early, four a.m. – not that he'd gotten much sleep to begin with. As the chill lessened, his body slowly began to relax. He opened his eyes and saw two more staring at him from the other side of the shower door. "Pervert."

As if in response, the orange cat lifted its hind leg and began licking where his testicles had once been.

"Showoff," Jerry said and proceeded to wash his own in a more acceptable way.

The cat lifted its head and looked at him as if to say, *you know you're jealous,* then meowed.

Not for the first time since remodeling the bathroom the previous summer, Jerry regretted having installed a see-through shower door. He'd felt the same way ever since opening the back door to the deck and watching in disbelief as the half-starved cat scooted between his legs and into the safe confines of the house. Jerry had told the cat at the time it was only temporary. Apparently, the cat didn't believe him. Six months later the cat, who Jerry still referred to as Cat, was still here, amazing since Jerry had never considered himself a cat person. Jerry finished his shower and opened the door to relieved meows. As soon as Jerry stepped out of the shower, Cat leaped from the counter and rubbed against Jerry's still wet legs, singing a mix of soft mews and purrs. Jerry snapped the towel at the cat, who turned and snagged the edge of the towel in one of its nails. *You're on borrowed time, Cat.* As Jerry untangled the paw, the cat pulled back, cutting a single scrape across the back of Jerry's hand. *It was so much easier when he lived alone.*

Jerry dressed in sweats, then made his way down the hallway and into the kitchen. The smell of freshly brewed coffee greeted him as he entered the room. *What did people do before timers?* He poured a cup, then moved to the table. The cat jumped onto the table. Jerry scooped him up and placed him on the floor. "Stay off the table, Cat."

The cat meowed his discontent.

"Remember, Cat: my house, my rules. And my rules state that I do not have to feed you until after I have had my morning coffee."

He took a sip of coffee, grateful for its warmth. It had been two days since the blizzard incident, and he still had trouble getting warm. Not that the icy shower had helped, but at least he was now fully awake. Both parties involved in the accident were going to recover fully, and Holly was going to keep her leg. He smiled just thinking of her. He reached for his cell phone, thinking to call and ask her how she was feeling this morning, remembered the time, and returned the phone to the table. *Easy, Jerry; you keep this up, and people might get the wrong impression.* "Can't have that now, can we?" he said, picking up the neglected stack of unopened mail.

He sifted through the stack, tossing the obvious junk to the side. He came to a business envelope and paused. The envelope was addressed to Trooper Jerry McNeal, with no return address. He looked closer at the postmark, which showed Michigan. To some, this would appear to be spam, but the hairs on the back of Jerry's neck told him otherwise. He took another sip of coffee before tearing into the envelope and pulling out its contents.

Dear Mr. McNeal,

A friend of mine was visiting Gettysburg last month and happened to stumble upon an article about you in one of the local papers. Forgive me for not knowing which paper, as my friend did not think to save the whole paper, instead just clipping the article in which your story appeared. Carrie, that is my friend's name, was fascinated when she read about what you described as your feelings. Carrie knew I would be interested, so she saved the article for me. I've had the article for several weeks, not meaning to do anything about it, until now.

My daughter, Max —at least that's what she calls herself; it's short for Maxine, although why she'd prefer to go by a boy's name instead of the beautiful name of her great-grandmother, I'll never know. Please forgive me for rambling. I just am not sure what I need to say to you. Oh, the hell with it, I will just tell you what is on my mind. Max also has "those feelings." Sometimes, they come to her in a dream. Other times, she just seems to know things. There have also been times when she doesn't know what is wrong, but she is uneasy for days until "it" happens. So far, they've been small things, well, most of the time. Anyway, over the past week, my daughter has been having a recurring dream that involves someone being killed. I cannot very well walk into our local police station and tell them this as they would surely have me committed, and where would my daughter be then? Please, Mr. McNeal, I need to ask you, knowing what you know (that the feelings

are indeed real) what would you do in my place?
My daughter is twelve years old.
Mrs. April Buchanan
810-555-5555

Jerry reread the letter twice before placing it back in the envelope. He knew the article of which the woman spoke. He'd not been happy when his sergeant insisted he give the interview. Since the story's release, Jerry had gotten multiple letters, all telling him about their feelings, some even telling what they thought of his so-called feelings, but this one just felt different. Yes, okay, he had a feeling about it. He picked up the phone, debated about the early hour, and dialed the number. As his call was answered, and a young voice drifted through the receiver, that feeling intensified...

Sherry A. Burton

*Join Jerry McNeal and his ghostly
K-9 partner as they put their gifts to good use
in:*

Ghostly Guidance
Book 2 in the Jerry McNeal series.

Please help me by leaving a review!

**Enjoy what you read? Please tell
EVERYONE!**

About the Author

Born in Kentucky, Sherry got her start in writing by pledging to write a happy ending to a good friend who was going through some really tough times. The story surprised her by taking over and practically writing itself. What started off as a way to make her friend smile started her on a journey that would forever change her life. Sherry readily admits to hearing voices and is convinced that being married to her best friend for forty-one-plus years goes a long way in helping her write happily-ever-afters.

Sherry resides in Michigan and spends most of her time writing from her home office, traveling to book signing events, and giving lectures on the Orphan Trains.

Made in the USA
Las Vegas, NV
19 September 2023

77819220R00069